EN.

by

Stephanides

stephanides.author@gmail.com

Copyright © 2019 Stephanides

All rights reserved.

ISBN: 978-1-7938-8168-7

THE STRANGER

I knew the house was a shithole the second I saw it, but I decided to take the room anyway.
What choice did I have? I had already seen three houses that day; all of them were shitholes and also way out of my price range. This house was the only affordable shithole I could find. It was barely accessible to public transport, the neighbourhood was strewn with litter and discarded furniture, the carpets were old and coarse, the bathroom ceiling was cultivating a black, sprawling mould, and my bedroom was pokey, dark, and exuded an odour of dust and decay. But I just had to accept it; this was now my home.
I was moving because the landlord at my previous house had made the sudden decision to renovate the place and double the rent. He was probably inspired after watching one of those property shows on television. Get the hipsters and professional-types in, those fuckers will pay anything. We, the low-life, transient, bedsit-scum

were no longer good enough for him. He gave us two weeks to clear out our things and find alternative accommodation. We didn't kick up a fuss. There was nothing that we could do anyhow. No-one to complain to, no action to take, no case to be heard. Well, even if there was, we didn't bother trying. It was far easier to just accept the landlord's whimsy and move on. I had experienced this type of thing before. It was simply part of life, moving from one shared accommodation to another.

I don't think I managed more than a year at any one place. Sometimes, it was because I was thrown out, but usually I would move out of my own accord. In these places, it would reach the point where I couldn't stand living there any longer. For instance, in one houseshare, a tenant would greet me with a fist-bump every time I passed him - every fucking time. It didn't matter if I was on the way to my bedroom, in the middle of making food, or going to the toilet to take a piss, if he saw me he would insist on the fist-bump - it was pathological.

Another time, I moved out because one of the other tenants always left the door to his room open. His room was immediately opposite mine and he would just sit watching streaming sites on his laptop all day, every day. Every time I emerged out of my room, I would be greeted with the soles of his disgusting feet perched on his desk as he stared glassy-eyed into his screen. It drove me mad.

I also left a place because one of the tenants coughed incessantly. At first, I didn't think much of it, but by the third month, it pushed me over the edge. That horrible rasping sound! I couldn't stay there any longer.

It's tough living with a bunch of strangers all the time. I despise small talk and pleasantries, particularly around the house. I just want to be left to my own devices. I have no interest in learning more about their lives or becoming friends. I see no purpose in it. Their stories mean nothing to me. They are all the same. If I could have lived on my own, I would have, but I couldn't afford such a luxury, particularly with my shitty low-paid job. I was a picker for online orders in a supermarket warehouse, and that's all you need to know; let's face it, there is nothing more to know.

I was stuck in that hellish cycle of houseshare to houseshare to houseshare. It was a doomed existence, and all I really wanted was some peace and quiet. Over time, I taught myself to accept my fate, and learnt to bottle up my contempt for the other tenants, as it was pointless to allow the minutiae of everyday existence to affect me. I had to be resilient. I had to ignore my neighbours, not simply tolerate them. I had to actively ignore that they existed. I did everything in my power to try and achieve this. Since I had begun the cycle of living in houseshares, I had become a master of avoidance and covert living. I knew all the tricks that ensured that any contact with the other tenants was minimised as much as possible. So, when I moved into this new house, I immediately put all my techniques into action.

I had my four duffel bags with me, which contained all my worldly possessions. As a transient, I needed to be minimalist, economical. I had to think about the logistics of constantly moving around from one place to another. Also, the rooms in which I lived rarely provided ample storage space - usually a maximum of one cupboard. So, if I bought something new, it had to replace something old. If I bought a new pair of jeans, then an old pair of jeans would need to go. There was no room for sentiment. Each duffel bag had its own specific function. The first duffel bag was for clothes. The second duffel bag was for underwear, towels, and shoes. The third duffel bag was for my laptop, bathroom accessories, and miscellaneous items. Finally, the last and most important duffel bag contained the fruits of my only worldly interest - an assortment of dried and preserved insects displayed in either acrylic resin blocks, glass frames, amber, or jars of rubbing alcohol. Some of them were rare and expensive like the *Zelotypia stacyi* or the *Callipogon Orthomegas monnei*, but the majority were common and easy to find on any collectors site. However, they were all special to me and the only housemates that I truly needed.

I unpacked all my stuff. I jammed my clothes and other items into the cupboard, which took no more than a few minutes, and then proceeded to carefully place the insects on the desk and wall mounted shelf provided. I thought it was typical that a desk would be provided with no accompanying chair. This house was no different from all the other houses in which I had lived. It had been redesigned to squeeze in as much bedroom space as possible. Originally, it must have been a regular

Victorian terrace house with three bedrooms, but it was now filled with six rentable bedrooms. The living room on the ground floor had been split down the middle to create two bedrooms, and the now-cramped bathroom on the first floor had obviously been compromised to fit a small bedroom alongside. The only communal space was the kitchen, which was green and ugly and had a table with six flimsy plastic chairs around it - one for each tenant, I presumed.

After I had unpacked all my stuff and displayed all my insects the way I liked them, I laid on my bed and took a nap.

I managed to last for at least four hours before running into the first tenant. I went to the kitchen to make some toast. He must have been waiting to catch me, because as soon as I slotted that bread in the toaster, I heard him come out of his room and scurry downstairs. I rolled my eyes at the thought of having to suffer the ensuing pointless exchange, but I knew it was something that just had to be done.

I turned my back to the kitchen door as I knew that this would make it harder for him to initiate the conversation. When he entered the kitchen, he stood there for a few seconds waiting for me to turn around, but I didn't. He coughed, but I remained motionless. He finally tapped me on the shoulder and I had no choice but to turn around.

He introduced himself as Pablo. I told him my name was Nilos. He asked if the name was English. I said no it wasn't. He asked me what I thought of the place. I shrugged. He started asking about the area and if I was familiar with the neighbourhood. I said it's London, it's all basically the same shit: houses, roads, shops, and cars. He proceeded to divulge his life story to me. But, as he started to recite his spiel, the toaster popped, giving me the excuse to say that my toast was done and it was time for lunch. I quickly returned to my room.

During the first few days, I met all the other tenants living in the house. One by one, they introduced themselves to me, and I duly gave each of them the cold shoulder. However, I was aware that there was a fine line; I couldn't be too rude, otherwise it could cause an altercation, so I had to be just rude enough so that they were aware that I was not the kind of person with whom they wanted to converse. People came and went in these types of places so frequently that it didn't matter who you offended anyway.

I learnt the times that all they left for work, and also studied their bathroom and kitchen routines so that I could effectively avoid them. Nothing is worse than being disturbed mid-shit or having someone try to start a conversation while cooking pasta. The best way to avoid this was to learn the habits of the other tenants and plan my day accordingly. In many ways, I perceived the others in the house as insects - they were slaves of function and instinct. Even the messiest and most disorganised of tenants still had a routine, they just weren't aware of this fact. If you studied their movements intimately, then you could predict them with a fair amount of precision. People like to think they're unique or special in some way, but they are not. Everyone is the same, more or less - like insects.

Another strategy I employed to avoid contact with the others was to use the communal spaces as quickly as possible. I'd never cook an elaborate meal, only simple and fast meals with minimal cleaning required. The faster I was done and out of that kitchen, the less chance there would be of running into one of the others. I would cook thin pasta, small chicken strips that could be fried in five minutes, microwaveable rice packets, and sauces from jars that would take only minutes to heat. On no account would there be roasts, casseroles, or salads with a multitude of vegetables and ingredients. Food was for sustenance only; I never bothered with taste - it was irrelevant. If the finished meal didn't induce a feeling of nausea, then it was a success.

Unfortunately, there were times when I would unavoidably come into contact with one of the others; there was always going to be some level of unpredictability in their behaviour. In this eventuality, I would simply greet them with a pleasantry, and as soon as they replied, I'd follow this up with a strained smile then walk out of the room. If it happened in the middle of cooking and they came into the kitchen to cook or chat, that was trickier. Usually, in that situation, I'd just have to take the hit. On a good day, I would brave the conversation, but if it was a bad day, then I'd leave the meal undercooked and eat it half raw; in fact, most of my meals were designed to be eaten that way just in case I found myself confronted with such a situation.

It wasn't ideal having to live in this manner all the time; in fact, it was frustrating and consumed significant time and effort. But, I had become accustomed to it over the years, and by the time I got to this house, it was second nature. I just did it unconsciously, and within a month of living there, I knew everyone's cycles and managed to continue my existence by only barely interacting with them. And, if I did happen to bump into them, they knew I was not a person with whom they wanted to converse. I had made that house my home. I thought I had the others sussed - they were predictable and stupid. However, this was only until Guy entered the picture. I could never have prepared to meet a tenant like Guy, and I never thought someone could infiltrate my life the way he did.

*

It was about the fifth week into my tenancy. The person in the room next to mine had decided to move out. One morning, I opened the door to my room and was confronted with a mess of boxes and bags in the hallway, which were blocking my passage. I attempted to step over the pile, which I could've done with no trouble, but when the tenant saw me, he insisted on moving it all out of the way. And, as he was shuffling his things around trying to make a space for me to pass through, he told me that he was moving on. He said it in a way that anticipated I would be saddened by the news, but of course, I couldn't have cared less. He told me that he had finished his university course and that he was moving back to Ireland, or Scotland, or Australia, or some shit, and that he was sorry that he hadn't had the chance to get to know me better. I told him coldly that I was sad to see him go and then walked off as he was trying to give me his parents' address to which we could forward his post. There was no way I was about to agree to that nonsense, so I pretended that I didn't hear him and escaped from the house as quickly as I could. I had seen so many tenants come and go in my life that I knew all the kinds of things that they would ask upon leaving. The worst one was when they asked for help with their move, or at least to help carry their stuff down to the van. To me, there was no greater imposition than having to help someone move their things. When I first began house sharing, I would allow myself to get embroiled in it, not knowing how to decline their requests. But, over time, I learnt that the best way to avoid it was to just bluntly say that I gad no interest in helping them. Who cares if they thought I was an arsehole? They would be gone by the next day anyway.

I went to work and came home as usual. When I got home, I saw that the room next to mine still had boxes and bags blocking the hallway, although they were now the possessions of the new tenant, who was in the process of moving in. The turnaround was quick in this place, I thought, as I climbed over the boxes while trying not to be noticed by the new tenant. Nonetheless, he quickly spotted me as I heard an emphatic "Hi!" emanate from his room, which I duly ignored. I continued into my room and closed the door.

I changed out of my work clothes and into my loungewear, ready for a night of reading about the lives and bodies of insects. That night, I intended to research a recently discovered species of ant found in Cambodia. I had also decided to skip dinner, as I did not want to risk getting into a conversation with the new tenant. I knew what the new ones were like; if you bump into them on the first day, then you will be subjected to at least an hour's worth of introductory conversation, and I was not in the mood for that.

I sat on my bed, opened my laptop and started on my research, but I was continually distracted by mumbling from the room next door. The new tenant was talking to some of the other tenants from the house. I couldn't relax; it felt as though I was involved in the conversation myself. All I could hear was strained laughter, positive sentiments, and getting-to-know-you chit-chat. The stuff of nightmares.

Soon, the other house tenants had also found their way into his room and they were all involved. They were bonding - and I was losing it. I just couldn't concentrate on my research anymore, so I slammed my laptop shut, curled up on my bed and waited for the conversation to end. Only, the conversation didn't pass, it went on and on. Then, the worst of all - I heard a knock. A knock on my door. On *my* door!

At first, I didn't open it, but the problem was they already knew I was home. Regardless, I thought that if I didn't answer it, then they would get the message that I didn't want to be disturbed. They didn't get this message and promptly knocked again, and then again - each knock becoming increasingly harder and louder. After the fourth knock, I got off my bed and opened the door. Now, when I think back to that moment, I know that I shouldn't have opened the door. I should have ignored it. I should have made it clear that I didn't want to be disturbed. I should have put a pillow over my head and pretended they weren't there. I should have jumped out of the fucking window. But, I experienced a lapse in judgement, and I did open that door.

Behind the door stood the new tenant. He was tall, athletic, and had a huge beaming smile; he looked like he had been ordered from a glossy lifestyle catalogue.

"Hi, I'm Guy," he said.

He stuck out his hand for a shake so I reluctantly offered a limp hand in return, which he seized with a vice-like grip. Helplessly, I winced as my fingers were crushed together. He looked me straight in the eyes as he shook my arm aggressively. He then asked me my name and I told him that it was Nilos. He asked me if he could call me Nil for short, but I didn't answer. He blathered on about what a great bunch of tenants lived in the house and that he was chuffed to be there and that he was sure we were all going to have an amazing time together. I said that all sounded great, while slowly nudging the door closed. He propped his elbow up against the door to counteract my slow retreat and then asked me the dreaded question - did I want to go to the pub with everyone for a drink and a chat? No, I did not, and I informed him as such. But it didn't deter him; instead, it only served to increase his determination. He grabbed me and brought me close, putting his arm around my shoulder.

"Come on, bro, everyone is going," he said. "It won't be the same without you."

I offered every excuse I could think of: I need to get up for work tomorrow, I'm feeling tired, I don't have anything to wear, I'm not in the mood. But, as I was saying these things, his eyes just glazed over and with that dumb smile frozen on his face, he would say, "Come on, bro. Just one drink," after every excuse that I made. When my list of excuses was exhausted, we just stood there staring each other down. Finally, when the face-off became unbearable, I broke and consented to come along for one drink — just one drink. He threw his arms up and cheered, then put his hand out for another finger-crushing shake, to which I begrudgingly complied.

He called out to the other tenants who were waiting in the kitchen downstairs, "He's coming! Leave in five minutes!" He turned back to me and reiterated gravely, "five minutes", and walked off to wait in the kitchen with the others.

I went to my wardrobe and put on some jeans and a T-shirt. I almost made the effort to improve my appearance, and then I remembered that I couldn't give a fuck. I was changed and downstairs in less than two minutes. When I walked into the kitchen, Guy remarked, "You took your time. What were you doing? Putting on your makeup?" The other tenants all howled with laughter. Guy had a can of beer in his hand. He offered me a sip, but I declined. He shrugged and then quickly downed the rest. He belched before instructing the "troops" to get moving to the pub.

On the way to our destination, I learnt the names of the other tenants, even though I knew all their names anyway. There was Pablo, who I had met on the first day, and there was also Loz, Oscar, and Will. They all told me where they were from and what they did for work/studying, but I wasn't listening. It made no difference to me. You can be from anywhere you like, it doesn't make you any more or less interesting to me.

The walk to the pub was short and from the outside it looked as every other pub. I didn't drink alcohol and I was not a frequenter of pubs. Even so, my perception was that this one was the same as the rest - a depressing shithole full of loud, drunk arseholes. In spite of this, the others in the group seemed to approve of the place. I couldn't understand what they were all seeing and just put their affirmation down to hollow positivity. No-one could honestly think that being in here was good - surely?

Guy led the way to the bar and instantly attracted the attention of the bartender.

"Right, what are we all having?" Guy asked.

Loz, Oscar, Pablo and Will all "ummed" and "ahhed" and took their time in choosing different varieties of beer. What's the fucking difference? They are just different versions of diluted alcohol, I thought. And, when they had all finally ordered their craft lagers or obscure pale ales, Guy looked at me and asked me what my "tipple" was. I informed him that a glass of water would be fine. They all laughed at this. Apparently, it was a bad choice. I told him to put a bit of lemon in it to give it some flavour, but this also wasn't the right choice. The laughter was repeated.

"You've got to have some alcohol, bro!" Guy remarked.

I told him that I didn't drink alcohol and I also had work the next day. More laughter ensued. Guy told me to just have one drink, that it would be fine. I told him to just give me a pint of whatever he was having. Anything, I thought, just to shut them all up.

We took our pints over to a table and sat down. There was a brief awkward silence that was quickly broken by Guy. There was no way that he was going to allow the moment of social unease to continue, so he concocted some bullshit conversation starter like "What's the most you've ever drunk in one night?" or some other macho nonsense like that.

Now that the others were more relaxed, the dreaded happened - they began asking me about my past. I hated such questions. What was I meant to say? What version of my life was I meant to give them? I certainly wasn't going to tell them the truth. They did not want to know the truth; even I did not want to know the truth. I opted for the standard lie that I had lived an average life in an average way. They seemed bored by my answers.

However, Guy was a fucking natural. He kept the conversation moving and flowing with one idiotic conversation starter to the next. "What is the craziest party you've been to?" "How many countries have you travelled to?" "What's the longest time you've been without sex? No lying!!"

By the time everyone was on their third beer, they had all loosened up and were freely spouting bollocks. I was still only halfway through my first pint. It tasted disgusting and I had no desire to get drunk.

Pablo, who was sitting next to me, started telling me his whole life story about his life back in Spain and why he had come to England and how he was glad to have found a room in a house with such great people and that he couldn't wait to experience London and blah blah fucking blah. What the hell was I listening to? What was the point of listening to his story? I couldn't fathom what I was getting out of it apart from alcohol-soaked breath being spat into my ear.

The rounds continued to flow, and as the drunkenness increased, the louder they also became. The beers were constantly spilling from their glasses, creating a sticky pool of liquid on the table that slowly dripped off the edges and onto our legs. The others didn't seem to notice this irritating phenomenon, were perhaps used to it after frequenting pubs or just simply understood that it was all part of the pub experience.

They began recounting scenes and storylines from TV series' that they had watched. Laughter and anger were shared when recalling these storylines. Every series that they discussed seemed to have a ridiculously implausible premise, which they thought they were the most important, most amazing things that they had ever seen. I remained quiet, as I had no use for TV and similar types of media. Then, they discussed travel and all the places and things that they had experienced, all trying to outdo each other with their "amazing" life-altering experiences. They all agreed that everyone should travel, because it, like, opens your mind to so much more than just what you know, and like, there's this amazing full moon beach party that lasts all night. I also stayed quiet throughout this conversation, as it was no benefit to me. I had visited other countries before for short holidays, but had never participated in this "travelling" thing, which as far as I could tell was just an extended self-delusional holiday. Every other country I'd ever seen just seemed to me to be a slight variation to my usual experience of life and culture. Different ways of saying hello and different brands of crisps. What were they seeing that was so perception-altering? Did booze-tubing in Vang Vieng change their minds about the nature of life and existence?

Then, the conversation turned to films. Oscar was a superhero movie freak and thought that a man flying through the air or a man dressed up as a bat was the most important thing that's ever existed. His opinion was that these films told us about who we are and were filled with important metaphors and life lessons. Will disagreed; he liked the kind of art film where someone mumbles and goes on a life-changing road trip or some load of complete toss. Oscar was a horror man, preferring those films where a person's mouth is sown to another person's arsehole, which apparently reveal the true nature of humanity. As far as I could tell, they were simply arguing over the same three-act structure presented in a slightly different way. Then, Guy chimed in with his opinion.

"All of you are right," he said. "This argument just shows how profoundly touching and important film is. How it can crawl under our skin and affect our very soul. It shines a light on who we are and who we want to be, and what we expect of ourselves and others. Film resonates with our dreams and desires and puts us in tune with something untouchable or undefinable. Something divine. It doesn't matter what genre we discuss, they all come from the same fabric. The desire to understand the human condition in all its beauty and all its flaws. Our lives create film and film creates our lives. How can anyone not love it?! Films inspire me, and I love watching them. Just like all of you."

After he had finished his gushing appraisal of film, the others looked at him with dewy-eyed awe. They were obviously taken with his speech. I, however, had always personally found the film format to be profoundly dull. Insipid, even. But, I knew better than to voice this particular opinion, so when they asked what films I liked, I just told them I agreed with what Guy had said. And, when they asked what other things I liked, I just said, yeah, travelling or whatever. There was no way I was to bother telling them the truth. Not because I was ashamed of it, but because I knew they wouldn't understand.

The truth was that I researched insects and tried to find out as much as I could about them. Not because I particularly took pleasure in the look of them. Quite the opposite; in fact, I found them disgusting and repulsive. But this is what drew me to them. Finding something this disgusting was the closest feeling to enjoyment and fascination I could achieve. It was at least an arousal of my senses, something that allowed me to create what I interpreted as a primal connection to them. Their purpose was that of function with no pretence. They fulfilled their purpose and then they died; there was something simultaneously noble and utterly base in that. I could relate to the insects. Or, probably and most simply, my studying of them was because I needed something to occupy my time and that was the least objectionable pastime I could find.

Anyway, I knew it was time to leave when Guy returned with a round of shots. I stood up and told everyone that it had been fun, but I really needed to get back, as I had to get up early and had a long day ahead of me. But, Guy wouldn't let me leave before we all did the shots. I covertly poured my shot into my half-drunk pint of beer and pretended to down it with the others. I departed immediately after. I don't think they even noticed me leaving, they were too busy engaging in mutual backslapping over their communal consumption of the shots.

I retreated into the cold night and felt relieved to have escaped from that environment. That was one of the worst nights I'd experienced in a long time, and I promised that I would never let myself get tangled in a social situation like that again. I don't know how Guy managed to convince me to go there in the first place. It must have been a lapse of judgement, but I wouldn't allow that to happen again.

*

I arrived back at my room and instantly felt at ease again. I lay on my bed and glanced at my jar of locusts. Disgusting things, but at least they were dead. Their bodies frozen in time for the pathetic amusement of one man - me.

I then turned my gaze to the jet black *Lucanus cervus* stag beetle which was encased in acrylic. I became mesmerised by the empty, lifeless holes that were its eyes. They resembled a void that now saw nothing and realised nothing. But, for a moment, the beetle seemed to stare back at me, returning the gaze. I saw myself through its eyes and I felt like the personification of the void; the deepest darkest chasm from which nothing escapes, where I and the beetle were one. I fell asleep with the beetle's eyes etched into my mind; they became the darkness that snuffed out my dreams.

However, the sleep was brief. I was soon awoken by the slamming of a door - it was the rest of the tenants arriving home from the pub, drunkenly shouting, laughing and clattering things about. I sprang up in my bed and looked at the beetle again. I wished that I could be in his place of rest; a place where it was impossible to be disturbed - encased in acrylic.

I listened to my housemates as they all talked over each other, vying for their voices to be heard. Guy's voice was the most piercing though, and the only one that I could hear with sufficient clarity to understand what was actually being said. The others' voices were just a cacophony of muffled vowels.

"Come on, lads. I can't wait to get stuck into these!" Guy bellowed.

A pungent smell of grease and charred meat began to waft through the house, so I assumed that Guy was referring to some takeaway food, probably kebabs, that they had bought on the way back, and now he was drumming up the anticipation of devouring them.

"This is what it's all about!" Guy added, as they settled in the kitchen to eat, drink and continue their incessant jabbering.

Later in the night, Guy shouted, "I know! I'll go and get my speaker and we can throw on some tunes!" I then heard him running up the stairs, entering his room, then quickly running back down again. "Got it!" he screamed at the others.

It wasn't long before the speaker was put into action and the music was blaring at full blast.

"Listen to this sick playlist!" Guy bragged.

A thick, bass-driven beat began to emanate from the kitchen, signifying that Guy's playlist had started. The walls vibrated to the bass, and I curled my fingers in anger.

Now, I was not interested in cultural tropes like film or TV or books or comedy, or whatever. But music, well, that was truly the worst. I had no taste for it at all. Its obnoxious musings were by far the most sickening aspect of society's self-gratification. And, whether it was pop, rock, rap, classical, opera, instrumental, a cappella, folk, dance, or whatever, it all sounded like dog shit to me. It was aesthetically no different to the muffled shouts and laughter of my annoying drunken housemates. But, its power to arouse such emotion and euphoria in people was something that I found truly bewildering, and also the most alienating aspect when attempting to connect with other people. Music's a thing that is adored without question. But, I questioned it, and I hated it. It was when I realised that I had no interest in music that I realised that I had no interest in other people.

After at least fifteen minutes of lying in my bed being prevented from sleeping by their vulgar noise, I decided that I would just have to go down and ask them to lower the volume. I hated confrontations, but it had to be done.

I opened the door to the kitchen and I saw Pablo slumped over on the table with his head resting in his arms, passed out from drinking excessive amounts of alcohol. Loz was gorging on the leftovers of everyone else's kebabs, while Will and Oscar were watching Guy as he pranced around the room miming the words to the song that was playing. He was in a hypnotic reverie dancing to the music and didn't notice my presence. In fact, none of them seemed to be aware that I was there. I approached Oscar and tapped him on the shoulder, but he didn't respond; he was either drunk or engrossed in Guy's performance.

When the song ended, and they finally noticed that I was standing among them, Guy looked at me and said, "Yo, Bro! Have you come to join the party?!"

I began to calmly tell him that the music was a bit loud and that I was having trouble falling asleep, but before I could finish what I was saying, the next song had already started, and Guy had begun dancing wildly again.

I noticed that Guy's phone was next to the speaker and was clearly the device that was transmitting the playlist, so I picked it up and shut it off. The music stopped abruptly and they all turned to look at me. I once again explained I had to get up early the next day and that the music was too loud.

Guy walked up to me and put his arm around my shoulder, drawing me into close embrace. "No worries, Nil, my man. We'll keep it down."

I thanked him and walked out. On the way back to my room, I heard them sniggering - a dig no doubt aimed in my direction. But I didn't care - as long as they kept the volume down, they could mock me all they wanted.

I got back into bed and looked at the time; it was nearing three a.m. I was tired, but found it hard to sleep as adrenalin was racing through my body.

I had barely slept at all by the time I had to get up for work the following morning. I woke up bleary-eyed, and even though I was already running late, I desperately needed a shower for a pick-me-up. But, when I entered the bathroom, the stench was worse than usual - there was puke everywhere, and it was making me gag. I decided to forgo the shower and just get a glass of water instead. I pulled on my workwear and went into the kitchen. The whole place was trashed. Beer cans and takeaway containers were strewn across all the surfaces and the sink was full of pots and pans as well as a thick red sauce that appeared to be an attempt at cooking a late night curry. Pablo was still passed out, sprawled across the table in exactly the same position as when I had made my feelings known to them all the previous night. He was snoring loudly and the air was thick with flatulence and sweat. I decided to just get a bottle of water on the way to work, as there was no way I was willing to navigate through that mess.

When I arrived at work, my boss remarked on how tired and dishevelled I looked. He concluded that I must have been out drinking the previous evening. He moaned that hungover workers were never a good thing. I didn't bother to fight my case, I just let him assume the worst of me and got back to work. Awful fucking work it was too. Irregular shifts and hours, sometimes no shifts, and tediously repetitive and mind-numbing work when it was available. But, there was no opportunity to find anything better. The friction I experienced in social situations meant I always ended up in low-paid and low-prospect jobs; jobs where it didn't matter if you were an outcast or a freak. In fact, looking at my co-workers over time, it became clear that being a freak or an outcast was actually a pre-requisite for those types of jobs.

Fuck it. I didn't care about money anyway. I wasn't a prolific consumer. But, what really stung was the knowledge that I could never afford to rent or buy a place of my own. My wages weren't even close to being enough for anything other than rent on a small room and food. Almost every penny was spoken for. I saved about twenty pounds a month, which had accumulated into a small amount of savings that merely acted as a safety net. It could never stretch to the purchase of a house or even a tiny flat.

At lunch, I sat on my own as I usually did. I hadn't had the chance to make myself sandwiches that morning due to the awful state of the kitchen and I wasn't going to pay for food in the overpriced canteen. So, I just sat there, ate nothing and stared into the distance; I wasn't disturbed once. People there knew not to sit next to me, or invite me to after-work drinks, or approach me for anything other than work-related matters. People came and went regularly in that place, so there wasn't much camaraderie or bonding anyway.

By the end of the day, I was really flagging and couldn't wait to get back to my room and have a long sleep. I hoped that by the time I got back, everything would have been cleaned and I could just quickly make some dinner and then go to bed. I was starving as I hadn't eaten anything all day. Even if the kitchen was still a mess when I got home, I would just have to brave it and make myself something regardless, I thought. But, the scenario I was confronted with in the kitchen when I returned home was far worse than just a mess, and far worse than I could have ever expected.

*

All the housemates were in the kitchen when I arrived home. They were chopping, slicing and rattling pots and pans, with an array of herbs and spices laid out on the table. The stench of raw seafood filled the air and glasses of white wine were being swirled and sipped by all.

Guy noticed me standing slack-jawed in the doorway. He approached me and ushered me into the kitchen. "Nil, my boy. You're home!" he said. "Just in time to help us with this magnificent meal. It's a paella! Courtesy of our Spanish master chef - Pablo!"

Pablo looked up at Guy and coyly smiled at the compliment. He raised his glass to Guy and then returned to his chopping.

"This is amazing, isn't it?" Guy prattled on. "I love food, don't you? Love it, love everything about it! I'm a real foodie, me. It's extraordinary how a certain flavour can enchant your senses. Just a simple taste of a dish can transport you to another place, another time. With one bite, I can be transported to the cobbled streets of Rome, dining alfresco in the warm sunshine. Or, I can be whisked away to a bustling food market in Bangkok eating noodles from a neon-lit stall. Sometimes, it can just take me to somewhere from the past, somewhere comfortable; maybe to my Grandma's house on a lazy Sunday afternoon as she serves up her famous roast. Extra Yorkshire puds for me, of course! This intangible connection we have with flavours is truly beguiling and, dare I say it, spiritual. And now, what an honour that we get to make an authentic paella de marisco! Put an apron on, get yourself a glass of wine and start chopping, amigo!"

Before I could protest, Guy had already draped an apron over my head and handed me a glass of wine. I stood there dumbstruck. Never as an adult had I felt so helpless when deciding my own actions.

He ushered me to a chopping board with a onion, ready to be diced, and suddenly transformed into business mode. "Oh yeah, seeing as we factored you in for the meal, you owe us twelve-pound-forty for the ingredients. We would've texted to clear it with you, but none of us had your number, but we were sure you'd want to be involved anyway."

Guy stared at me, which made me feel uneasy and pressured. I took a few steps back, took the apron off, put down the glass of wine and backed away from the onion on the chopping board. I informed him that It was all very nice of him and the others, but I had already promised some friends that I would meet them for dinner, and that I had only come home quickly to change out of my work clothes. Guy just continued to stare at me. I said that as they couldn't contact me, I didn't mind contributing my share of the money for the ingredients. So, I took fifteen pounds out of my wallet and handed it to him saying not to worry about the change.

"No probs, amigo," Guy said routinely. "We'll catch you next time."

I scurried out of the kitchen and went to my room. I changed out of my work clothes and hurriedly put on the first clothes that I could find.

As I walked out the house, I peered back into the kitchen and saw them all with their phones taking selfies while holding the king prawns up next to their faces. They were pulling comical faces at the prawns and were all rolling about with laughter. Their eyes were as hollow as the dead black eyes of the prawns with which they were posing. I grimaced at the sight and then got the fuck out of there.

I was so hungry, but I didn't know what to eat. I didn't usually order takeaway food and I had just given Guy fifteen pounds for a meal that I wasn't even going to eat, which had blown my budget. I roamed the streets for a bit and then saw that a fried chicken restaurant was offering six chicken wings for a pound, so I entered. I ordered ten chicken wings and some fries. I negotiated with the man behind the counter and managed to get the whole meal with a drink for only two pounds.

There was a small greasy seating area located at the front of the shop, so I decided to dine in. I brushed the previous customer's crumbs off the table with my sleeve and sat down. I needed to waste as much time in there as I could. I didn't want to go back home and end up getting involved with my housemates' little cooking party. For starters, no fucker could ever make me take a selfie with a king prawn, that was for sure.

I nibbled each chicken wing, trying to get the most out of the meal as I could, and I observed people coming into the shop to order their helpings of that putrid fried chicken. What an ugly bunch of fuckers were passing through that chicken shop, all ordering the same meal and in the same way. They had the same jokes, same chitchat, same voice.

Analogously, I spotted a small, plucky cockroach roaming around on the sticky floor. It was far less predictable than the humans that towered above it. It scuttled around the floor, expertly dodging the crushing feet of the customers above and seemed to be on a wild hunt without any specific purpose. It explored the gaps between the bolted-down table and the tiled floor. It scaled the walls and squeezed into the crevices in the light fittings, while the people below followed the same path to the counter and received the same chicken and spoke the same words. That cockroach's life was of more interest to me. What was it looking for? Where was it going? What was its endgame in all of this?

The allure of that creature was that it asked none of these questions and it wasn't expecting answers. It simply did what it did without thinking. So, how could it be working on that level, yet still be leading a more interesting existence than the humans that trudged around above and below it?

My musings were interrupted when I noticed that the chicken man behind the counter was staring at me. It was a get-the-fuck-out-of-my-shop kind of a look. I had outstayed my welcome, and to him, it must have looked like I was on drugs or something. What other reason was there for being mesmerised by an insignificant insect climbing the walls?

I left the shop and meandered through the streets for as long as I possibly could before I got so fed up that I just had to go home. Also, that fried chicken wasn't sitting well, and I desperately needed a shit. I glanced at my phone and noted that I had been absent for just over three hours, which must have allowed them more than enough time to cook and eat that fucking paella and all be safely back in their rooms.

I arrived back at the house and slowly inched the front door open. My heart sank when the first thing that greeted me was the sound of communal laughter and merriment. They were all in Loz's room, which was the front bedroom of the house on the ground floor. The door was wide open, and all the housemates were squeezed inside playing a football game on Loz's game console. They were cheering and acting like supporters at a real football match.

I tried to sneak past the room unnoticed, but it was pointless. They spotted me instantly and tried to get me to play the game. I declined and said that I was just going to bed as I was very tired.

"Hey. Hey. Nil! We left you some paella in the fridge! Go and try it. It's the fucking bomb, Bro!" Guy called out.

Then, the others cheered, and I wasn't sure whether the cheer was for the paella or for a goal one of them had just scored.

I didn't take much note of Guy's comment, but as I passed the kitchen to go upstairs, I stopped in my tracks. I have to admit, the idea of that paella captivated me for the briefest of moments, and I did wonder what all the fuss was about. But, I continued to my room and tried to get some sleep despite the sounds of obnoxious whooping that were emanating from Loz's room downstairs.

*

I woke up the next morning in a pool of sweat. It was another rough night's sleep. Perhaps I had suffered tormented dreams in the night; I didn't know. I could never remember any of my dreams.
I went to the bathroom, showered the sweat off my body and then got ready for work. I arrived at work early and put in an enthusiastic and proactive shift to demonstrate to the manager that I was an invaluable member of the team. But, he didn't notice any of my efforts. He only ever noticed when I did something wrong, which was the nature of these fuckers who were in charge.
By lunchtime, I had given up on trying to impress the manager. There was no point, it was just wasted energy. I got myself a cup of water from the cooler and a cereal bar from the vending machine and found a vacant table where I could sit. All I could think about as I sat there was the current situation back at the house. The entire scenario was irritating and I had never come across someone as vociferous as Guy before. He had forced his personality on that house so seamlessly and I was powerless to resist. The other housemates were willing victims and were enthralled by Guy and his attitude to life. All my little devices and timetables aimed at avoiding the other housemates would be useless if they were in the house all the time with all the doors open. I had

never planned for that type of scenario and I didn't know how long I would be able to tolerate living there. I contemplated moving out, but rents were becoming increasingly expensive and I had already been lucky to find that room. I just had to make the best of the situation whether I liked it or not.

After work, I trudged slowly home, deciding to walk the long distance instead of taking the bus. I dreaded to think what might await me in the house. I just hoped that they weren't all in the kitchen again, cooking up some huge meal like the previous day. I had no desire to walk the streets for hours and eat in that chicken place again.

When I finally got home, they were all in the kitchen preparing another meal. I gritted my teeth and suppressed the rising anger. They were playing music while they cooked, which meant that I was fortunately able to creep past the kitchen door and upstairs without anyone noticing my presence. I snuck into my room and quietly closed the door behind me. I laid on my bed and wondered what I was going to do about food. I was starving, but all my food was in the kitchen and there was no way that I could go in there with the others already occupying the space.

I waited and waited for them to vacate the kitchen. But, after they had finished their meal, I heard them decide to play a card game together - poker I think. I realised that they would be camped in the kitchen for the long haul that night and that I was just going to have to go without dinner. But, I was so hungry that I just couldn't relax, so I searched my room for something, anything, to eat. I looked at my insects and wondered if any of them were edible. I searched on the internet to see if this was a possibility, but didn't find any information on it. I suppose it wasn't a common occurrence for someone to want to eat their dried-out souvenir insects. I gave up on my search - there was nothing to eat in my room. From downstairs, I heard Guy shout, "Full house, bitches!" I imagined punching him square in his smug face.

Why did he have to choose this house out of all the others in London? Why couldn't he have rented a room somewhere else? Was he sent here solely to torture me?

I laid back on my bed, stared at the ceiling and thought of ways of resolving this situation. The first thought I had was to kill the lot of them, but I knew that this was too extreme. This was also my second thought, and although it sounded better the second time around, it still appeared not to be a feasible option. I then looked at my insects again and pondered. I stared deep into their lifeless eyes and I thought of the insect class as a whole; their adaptability, resilience and tenacity. They had a remarkable capacity to survive in harsh environments. They exhibited all the attributes that I would need if I was going to survive in that house; the harshest of all environments. I too would have to adapt and become tenacious.

I didn't have work the next day, so I began the process of putting my adaptation plan into action. I went to a huge outlet store that sold cheap household goods and bought a portable electric cooking hob, a kettle, a toaster, a cooking pot, a pan, a plate, a bowl, a cup, a wooden cooking spoon, cutlery, a chopping board and a plastic storage box. I took all the new items back to the house, dumped them in my room, and then headed out to the budget supermarket. There, I bought tins of beans, Spam, mackerel, soup, corn, peas, and other foods that could be stored under my bed and last indefinitely without being refrigerated. I also bought eggs, tea bags, bread, and a five-litre bottle of water.

I took all newly purchased goods home and set them up in my room. The space in the room was just about enough to accommodate all the stuff, even though it was a bit cramped. I was happy with what I had bought, but it had done some considerable damage to my savings. It also made a mockery out of my policy to only ever own a limited amount of possessions at any given time. And yet, I had no other choice, I would just have to accept the situation.

I decided to test my new gear by making egg on toast with a cup of tea. The portable hob didn't get very hot so the eggs took a bit longer, but overall, it was adequate. I also had to cook with the window wide open so that the heat and smoke could escape, which was fine as summer was approaching.

After it was all ready, I sat on my bed and ate my bedroom-cooked egg on toast. It was okay. When I had finished, I looked at my dirty plate and kitchen utensils and thought about how I was going to clean everything up; I didn't want to have to go down to the kitchen to achieve this. I decided to use the plastic container and some water from the five-litre water bottle, then after took the dirty water to the toilet and poured it away. Job done. But, I knew that in the future, I would have to devise a more sustainable option regarding the water. I knew that it would be a pain to live like this, but for now, it would suffice - I could cope. As long as things didn't get any worse, I could manage.

*

Soon, every occupant of the house left the door to their room permanently open. They would shift breezily from one room to another, conversing loudly, joking, laughing, watching box sets, playing music, playing computer games, and generally making my life a constant struggle to find some peace and quiet. They would ask me if I wanted to participate in whatever activity they were doing at that time. I would always have an excuse planned, and it was now obvious to everyone that I had no intention of getting involved in their trivial activities. Regardless of this, they still incessantly pestered me with their requests for me to join them. It was as if my lack of desire to participate was so offensive and unfathomable to them that it must have been because I didn't understand the questions they were asking. My inactivity somehow threatened to invalidate their sense of enjoyment.

As their sociability grew, I retreated further and devised new and innovative ways of staying in my room and keeping my distance from them. I had rigged up a hose system up the outside wall of the house, which fed into my room through the window. There was one hose for the incoming water, which was connected to the outside tap in the back garden. This hose was clipped onto a plastic tub in my room that I would use to wash up dishes, brush my teeth, wash my hands, clean my body, and also to piss into. The second hose was the outgoing supply, which was routed out of my bedroom straight into a drain outside. This hose was fitted with a large funnel so I could pour the dirty water or piss from the plastic tub into the funnel and dispose of it down the drain. Obviously, flushing the piss out this way was not what a storm drain was originally designed for, but that was of no concern to me. Luckily, the back garden was an overgrown shit-hole, so no one ever used it and therefore never saw my makeshift plumbing system.

I had successfully managed to confine most of my tasks to my room, but I still wanted to take it further. I began to plan a rope system that I could use to abseil down the back of the house from my room to the garden, so I wouldn't have to use the front door. The plan failed when I couldn't work out what to attach the rope to that would support my weight. Also, I was sure I would eventually be spotted by the neighbours and be accused of attempted robbery or something, so I disregarded that idea.

One morning, I overheard the housemates talking about me. They must've thought I had left for work already as they were discussing my lack of integration into the houseshare. Apparently, I was making them feel uncomfortable with my withdrawal from the group dynamic. Guy was the one who was leading the conversation; he had all the others hanging on his words and agreeing with everything he said. He spoke in a reasonable and calm way, which ultimately disguised the bullish and uncompromising nature of what he was really saying. They reached the conclusion that they would confront me with these issues and try to get to the bottom of why I felt like I didn't want to be part of the group. There wasn't any fucking reason. I was just a miserable prick and I was happy with that.

I knew then that I had to move out. I had lost and there was nothing I could do about it. I would just have to use the remaining money I had saved and find another room somewhere else. I was still under contract for this room so I'd probably lose my security deposit. This would leave me skint with barely sufficient means to live, but I had no choice - the mob had spoken.

I needed to get to work, so I knew I'd have to pass them by on my way out. But there was no way I could stomach a confrontation like that at that point. The thought of it made me nauseous. I needed to leave the house, but how could this be done without them noticing? I revisited my abseiling idea and wished that I had not dismissed it with no attempt to install the equipment. I looked out the window and scanned the exterior of the house to see if there were any pipes that I could use to climb down. There weren't any close enough.

I judged the distance from my window to the floor outside and concluded that if I hung from my window and then let go, the drop wouldn't be excessive. So, the choices were either to face my disgruntled housemates or jump out of the window - I chose the latter.

I opened the window as far as I could. It was a sash window so it opened quite far, and also meant that there was a sufficiently long strip of window beading to which I could cling. So, I climbed out, grabbed onto the beading and then slowly lowered myself down the wall until I was just hanging. It was at that moment that I completely lost my nerve and realised what a dumb idea the whole thing was. I didn't have the arm strength to pull myself back up again and just hung, helplessly sweating with panic as my fingers slowly lost their grip.

It wasn't a long drop and the fall from the window to the floor probably took less than a second. But, to me, it felt as though I had fallen from the top of a skyscraper. I hit the floor and landed awkwardly on my ankle. The pain was immense, but I had to get out of there before any of the housemates saw me. I hobbled off through the back garden and into the alleyway that backed onto the property, subsequently finding my way to the street.

As soon as I made it to the street, I collapsed. The pain in my ankle was overwhelming. I took off my shoe and sock and assessed the damage; it was already beginning to swell like a balloon.

I called work and informed my boss that I wouldn't be able to make it in that day. He expressed his extreme dissatisfaction and insinuated that I was lying to get out of work because I was hungover. I was in too much pain to argue my case, so I just hung up and endured the excruciating walk to the bus stop.

I had changed buses twice by the time I finally reached the Accident and Emergency department at the hospital, by which time my ankle was swollen to the extent that it couldn't fit in my shoe and resembled the colour of an aubergine.

I sat in the hospital for hours waiting to be seen; no-one seemed to give a fuck about me or my problem. Apparently, a swollen ankle is not a priority in terms of urgency. I watched as patient after patient was called in ahead of me to see the doctor. I suspected that they were all over-exaggerating their ailments in order to manipulate their way to the front of the queue. They were coughing and spluttering, spilling blood, howling in pain and moaning loudly, which made the waiting room resemble an evening at the am-dram. And, although I resented them for this spurious behaviour, I resented myself more for not thinking of that idea myself.

I desperately needed something to ease the pain, so I limped over to a vending machine and bought a can of Coke. I hobbled back to my seat and set the ice cold can against my ankle, which instantly provided relief. But, the can quickly turned tepid, so I decided I might as well drink it. I cracked it open and took a sip; it tasted like shit. I winced at its acidic, sugary shit-flavour. I placed it on ground and pushed it away from me. A man sitting opposite frowned at me like I had just rejected the nectar of the Gods.

Finally, I was called to see the doctor. Only, I didn't get to see the doctor; I saw a nurse who told me that it was simply a sprained ankle and that I needed to rest the leg, elevate it when sleeping and take some off-the-shelf painkillers if necessary. I asked him if I would be able to work with my ankle the way it was and he just shrugged and said it might be sufficiently healed in a couple of days. The advice was nothing more than I could have gleaned from a quick internet search. The whole trip had been a waste of time. It would have been better to hobble into work so my boss could at least see that I wasn't lying. Even so, he'd probably put the injury down to a drunken accident anyway.

There was nothing more I could do so I took the long bus ride home and prepared myself for the impending confrontation with my housemates, wishing that I just had the balls to face up to them in the first place. I would've saved myself a fucked-up ankle.

*

There must be an unwritten law that states that when someone is ill or injured, there should be no confrontations with that person, because when I limped through the door with my swollen ankle, they did not mention how they wanted me out of the house or that my presence was objectionable to them. Instead, they asked how the injury to my ankle happened, if I was okay, and if I had been to the hospital. I told them that I had had an accident at work and the hospital advised me to rest it as much as possible. They offered to bring me up a coffee and some food, but I politely declined and said that it had been a tough day and that I just needed some rest. They offered me a bag of frozen peas from the freezer to put on my foot and told me to call out for them if I needed anything. I thanked them, knowing I was never going to do such a thing.

I laid in bed and put a pillow under my foot to keep it raised and then balanced the bag of frozen peas on top of the swelling. I reached under my bed and pulled out a tin of Spam and tin of baked beans. I retrieved a fork from my bedside drawer, tore open the lids of the tins and had cold beans and Spam for dinner. After dinner, I did some reading on *Panesthia guizhouensis*, which was a new species of cockroach that had been found in China that only feasted on wood. I wondered if eating wood would have been tastier than the meal I just had consumed. I envied the animals that only ate one type of plant their whole lives; I was so bored with the multitude of foods and offerings that we as humans had to endure in the modern world. All the vitamins from all the different sources, all the fibre and fats and good cholesterol and bad cholesterol. Diets and dieting, healthy lifestyles and food fads. Organic, non-organic, locally sourced, free-range, hand-reared - what an unfettered superabundance of bullshit. I found the hype around food particularly vulgar. The culture of foodies and food was alien to me. If I could just eat wood and be done with it, that would suit me just fine. One taste forever and never know anything different. In juxtaposition to this, I could hear the others in the kitchen downstairs as they were making some sort of Asian-fused pork stew. They were swooning over all the ingredients and becoming more excited about the outcome than any grown man should ever get over a fucking pot of dead pig, water and vegetables.

I fell asleep listening to their unnecessary excitement and when I awoke the next day, I found that the peas had melted and a pool of water was congealing around my foot. The smell of last night's beans and Spam combined with the smell of the defrosted peas created one hell of a stench in the room. I shuffled over to the window and opened it as far as it would go to let the smell escape. I checked my ankle and the swelling had gone down slightly, but when I stood up, the pain was still intense. I called work and explained to my boss that I would not be able to make it in again. He was not pleased and abruptly hung up the phone. I took some photos of the bruising and swelling in order to demonstrate the damage to my boss when I eventually returned to work, but I was worried that this would not be enough to placate him.

There was a knock at my door. I shuffled to the door and cracked it open just enough for my face to show. It was Guy bearing a mug of tea. "Hey, my man," he said. "How's the old ankle?" I edged the door further open and stuck out my foot to show him. "Oooh. Still sucks balls, I see. But, look, I thought you might need this?" He held up the tea and offered it to me. "Take it. Looks like you could use a pick-me-up." I took the tea off of him and offered my gratitude. "No problemo, Amigo," he quipped. "Let me know if you need anything else."

I took the tea into the room and promptly poured it out of the window, then set out making my breakfast, which was basically the wet peas that had defrosted over my ankle the previous night. I simply boiled them until they had the consistency of a mushy paste. It was a hard meal to eat, but I thought of that wood-eating cockroach and approached the meal with the same mindset. Imagine if these peas were the only thing that I needed to eat to stay alive for the rest of my life.

I got back on my bed and dozed off while reading a book about the evolution of insects. I entered a weird state of sleep and hazed consciousness. My mind wanted to sleep, but the pain pulsating in my ankle kept my body awake.

A *Tenebrio molitor*, more commonly known as a mealworm beetle, flew in through the window and landed on my chest. I didn't know whether it was a dream or part of reality. It just perched itself on my chest and inspected me like I was the subject of its research. I waved my hands at it to swat it off, but I was dazed and kept missing, so I gave up and just let it stay there. I stared at it and it stared back at me with its beady black eyes and its feelers twitching and probing my bare skin. I was completely averse to touching live insects; studying them from a distance was fine, but actual contact I found to be off-putting. This particular one was stubborn and would not budge from its position on my chest. Was it trying to communicate with me? If I could speak insect, then I would ask it what it thought of humans. Were we as predictable as we seemed? Did insects think they were more intelligent than us? Were we as disgusting to them as they were to us?

The insect seemed to be urging me to close my eyes. To go back to sleep. To shut the fuck up with my questions.

Do insects not like questions?

Do they…

Are they…

I woke up in the late afternoon to knocking at my door again. For fuck sake, who was it now?! I had sweated profusely through my sleep and felt bewildered and disoriented.

I opened the door and it was Guy again. "Hey, man," he said. "Just seeing how you are."

I told him I was feeling a bit better, but my ankle still hurt. I was just resting it like the doctor had recommended. I said to him that it still needed more rest and then I began to close the door on him to signal that I just wanted to be left alone. But he was having none of that.

He wormed his way past the closing door and entered my bedroom uninvited. I was confounded by the audacity of this manoeuvre. No-one had ever entered my bedroom. This was my private space, it was not open to the public. He was a fucking trespasser as far as I was concerned and bile began to rise up my throat in anger, but I swallowed it down and watched him as he perused the room as if he was in a museum gift shop. The first thing that caught his eye was my collection of preserved insects.

"Woah, freaky shit," he said. "Some of these things look like they could be in a horror film. Look at this one! Look at its claws."

He meant it's mandibles. I told him that it was a *Lucanus cervus*, which was a common species, nothing to get worked up about. He wasn't listening to me though; instead, he continued to finger through my treasured collection, messing it up in the process. One by one, he picked them up and held them in the light coming from the window, inspecting them with facial expressions ranging from a grimace to slack-jawed wonderment.

"Quite a collection you have here, Nil," he said as he finished scrutinising the last one. "How long does it take to make a collection like that?" I didn't reply, so he answered his own question, "Yeah, probably a long time. Where do you even get these things anyway?" I didn't answer. "Well, of course, the internet. Get anything on the internet these days," he answered again.

He sat on my bed and for the first time, he noticed all my housemate-avoiding possessions. The fridge, the hob, the pots and pans, the makeshift taps. A strange look came over his face. This time, unlike when he was examining my insects, it was a sincere expression; unrehearsed, unconsciously made, real. It was a look of bewilderment and terror as if he had stepped into a serial killer's sanctuary. He was lost for words and started jabbering just to fill the awkward dead air with some sort of noise. "Me and the others were, er... er...

thinking of making burgers tonight. But, you know, actually making the burgers, not just cooking up some burgers bought from the supermarket. You know, getting stuck in and making the burgers from scratch. We thought it would be nice if you joined in. It could help you integrate into the group, get to know everyone. We're all good lads, you just need to spend some time to get to know us. I'm sure we will all get on… like a house on fire."

Like a house on fire. Those words stuck in my head.

I told him that my ankle was feeling pretty bad and that I didn't think I could walk around on it too much, but thanked him for the offer and said maybe next time. He was not accepting my excuse and was determined to get me to participate. "Don't be a total numpty," he said. "You can sit down. We'll pull up a chair and sit you right on it. You can have a beer and get involved. Happy days. It'll be a laugh." Awkward silence. "You can't stay in here all night. You'll go… mad. You need to socialise, get yourself out and about, mate." He paused for a moment and looked around at all the things in my room again. He seemed genuinely concerned. "This is not… It's not… You know, healthy. Living like this. Being like this. You need variety. Companionship. Friends. That's what makes life worth living. Surely?" He looked at me straight in the eyes. He could just not comprehend my way of life or my motives. I didn't know what else to say or do. His persistence was jarring and I wanted him to leave my room, so I agreed to come downstairs and help make those fucking burgers.

"Gonna be so much fun, you wait and see," he said as I hobbled out of my room towards the staircase with him following behind.

I panicked. What could I do to get out of doing this? I didn't want to spend my evening making burgers and listening to idle chit-chat from these wankers. I needed to think quick. Something. Anything!

I got to the stairs and was suddenly hit by an idea. It was a bad idea, but I had nothing else, so I did it anyway - I threw myself down the stairs. I rolled and tumbled pathetically to the bottom. It was a terrible show. The whole thing was slow and forced and undramatic.

Guy stood at the top of the stairs and looked down at me as I stared up at him. I said my foot had given way as it was obviously not ready to be walked on yet. There would be no way I could make burgers in such a state. I crawled up the stairs, groaning in pain as I did so. I crawled past Guy and back into my room; he was just watching me incredulously the whole way.

As soon as I reached the safety of my room, I closed the door and locked it. I straightened out all my misplaced insects and patted the imprint of Guy's arse out of the bedding.

I laid in bed and listened to the others downstairs as they pounded the meat into burgers. I knew my time in that place had come to an end. As soon as my ankle was better, I would have to find another place to live.

*

Three days passed before I was able to walk on my ankle again. Three days of lying in bed. Three days of sweat and Spam and cold peas. Three days of exile and solitary confinement. Three days of listening to the swirls of noise reverberating around the house courtesy of the other tenants. Three days of delirium and paranoia. Three days of avoiding the other housemates at any cost, even if it meant refraining from showering or shitting. I didn't want to confront them; I didn't know how to. I knew I had to leave the house. The situation had become untenable. Guy entering my room was the last thing that I could stomach. I had tolerated a lot in that house, but that was too much. I had lost and would just have to use the last of my savings to move to another place. I would lose my deposit on this room as it would involve breaking the contract, and this was going to have a huge impact on my finances. I could barely afford it, particularly after buying all the extra gear for my room. I looked at the fridge and the hob - what a waste of money they were, and now, instead of representing items of freedom, they had become a huge burden. How was I supposed to move all these new things to another place?

I wiped myself down with a flannel and water from the hose and got dressed for work. I looked around at the state of the room: the sweat-soaked bedding, empty tins of food and the heavy musk of an unwashed man. I realised that the odour must have been terrible, but I couldn't smell anything, I had become used to it.

Loz saw me leaving the house. He didn't say anything to me, but I felt his eyes boring into my back as I trudged out of the door. I briefly wondered what the other tenants must have thought of me until I quickly realised that I didn't give a shit.

When I got to work, my boss expressed his displeasure with my extended absence. I tried to explain to him about my ankle and showed him how purple and sore it still was. He said that if it still hurt, then I'd be no use to him at work that day and that I shouldn't have bothered coming in. Nothing I could say to him would placate him on the matter. He said that my shift for today had been filled anyway, so I should just go home. I asked him if he was firing me, and he just shrugged and said he wasn't allowed to do that if someone just took some sick days, but he added that my shifts would be reduced severely. He needed someone more reliable and I'd be contacted when they needed me. So, it basically felt from my perspective that I was being fired.

I slowly made my way home, wondering what the hell I was going to do. There would be no way I could find another place to live now. I needed my remaining savings to pay for rent and food. I couldn't afford to lose my deposit on this house and also pay out for another deposit on a new place. I calculated that if I remained where I was, then I had enough money for two to three months maximum. I decided that I had to stay in the house, even if the others wanted me to leave; I had no choice now. But, how was I going to deal with Guy? His presence there was more irritating than any other housemate I had ever had. That would be the toughest part of my predicament.

I got home and checked my supplies. I still had plenty of tinned food left and devised a plan determining how much I could ration each day to make the most of what I had. Every single penny had now become a vital component of my life. This scenario was exactly what my savings were for. I cursed that I had already spent a bulk of it on those other objects.

I cleaned up the room as it reeked; being out of that room and then returning to it brought my senses back to normal and exposed the festering hole it had become over the last few days. After I sorted everything out and sat down on my bed, I was struck by the gravity of the situation. A crushing feeling of depression suddenly consumed me and everything felt hopeless. People had always assumed that I was depressed as I didn't engage with things and didn't socialise. But that wasn't true. I was just indifferent and didn't care for "happiness". Over my life, I had tried to disengage with these insane ideas of enjoyment and happiness, and as I had never strived for these things, I also avoided the inevitable depression that accompanies the desire for such emotions. I tried to shake off the depression I was feeling by thinking as rationally as I could and planning a course of action that would enable me to escape from this house, but it was pointless. I laid on my bed and stared morosely at the ceiling. A fly was buzzing maniacally around the room trying to find something that was obviously not there. I wondered what it was looking for, or whether it was just pissed off that it's feast of Spam and pea leftovers had been cleared away.

I heard Loz, Guy and Pablo engaged in conversation in the kitchen. Their voices were muffled, but I could make out that Loz was telling them that he saw me going to work, so I must be better now. Guy asked if I was home and Loz said that he thought he heard me come back. Guy said he would go up to have a "chat" with me in a bit after he'd finished cooking his soup.

I was sick of all this shit. Why couldn't they just let me be and live how I wanted to live? What difference did it make to them that I stayed in my room? I never complained about them. I accepted that I hated them, but let them just get on with it regardless. I grew angry and decided that I wouldn't allow Guy the satisfaction of coming up to my room; I was going to be the one to confront them. I wasn't sure what I was going to say to them at that point; the adrenalin was blindly controlling my actions.

I exited my room and started to walk down the stairs, although my ankle still ached so I had to descend carefully. When I had made it to the kitchen, I peered in - it was empty. I heard cheers and commotion coming from Loz's room and realised that they must have gone there for a game of football on the games console. I noticed that Guy had left his pot of soup simmering on the hob. He had also left, very near to the hob on the worktop, a towel that he had been using.

An idea popped into my head - this is where I could really get my own back on Guy. I slid into the kitchen and moved the towel close to the simmering pot, just close enough to the flame. I slipped out of the kitchen as the sound of cheering came from Loz's room; one of them must have scored a goal, and for once, I knew what it must feel like to score a goal myself.

I crept back upstairs as quietly as I could and retreated into my room. It was almost as soon as I closed the door that all the fire alarms in the house started chiming with that ear-piercing sound. I heard the others rush out of Loz's room, panicking and shouting.

"It's coming from the kitchen!" I heard Guy scream.

I rushed out of my room and screamed out to them asking what was going on.

"Fire! Fire!" Guy shouted.

There was smoke billowing out of the kitchen. Loz was calling the fire department. None of them knew what to do. I rushed down the stairs as quickly as my ankle would allow and told them all to get out of the house. I battled through the smoke and into the kitchen, grabbing the fire extinguisher that was hung by the door off the wall. Then, I sprayed the extinguisher foam over the fire.

Soon the fire became only smoke. The others came into the kitchen and we inspected the damage. The hob had melted and the worktop had also sustained some fire damage. It wasn't too bad, but the cooker and part of the worktop would need replacing.

"I don't know what to say," Guy said meekly. "It was my fault. I must've left the towel too close to the hob and it caught fire. I'm so sorry. I'm just glad it wasn't worse."

Loz and Pablo told him not to worry about it. It was just an accident. They then praised me for my quick thinking, as it could have been much, much worse. I said I hadn't even thought about it, it just came instinctively.

"Yes, well done, Nil," Guy said begrudgingly. "We owe you big time."

I said I was just glad I had been there to help out and that we really needed to be careful when cooking from now on, and then I retreated back to my room.

That evening was bliss. There was no group cooking session, no PlayStation party, no music, no talking - there was just silence. Everyone stayed in their rooms and kept themselves to themselves, just how it should be in a houseshare of strangers. There was no need to engage or make bonds; the only need was to ignore each other's presence and get on with our lives. I revelled in the fact that I had successfully decimated their social unit, even if only for that night. If only it could stay like this forever, I hoped.

THE OUTCAST

Starting that fire had permeated a gloomy mood throughout the house and there was, for a while at least, peace and quiet. It was bliss. There were no mass evening cookouts or group activities of any kind. Everyone just stayed in their rooms and only conversed when bumping into each other in the hallway. The kitchen was mostly unusable as the cooker had been destroyed in the fire, so the tenants only used the kitchen to heat their individual ready-meals in the microwave.

Guy had become uncharacteristically subdued. He spent a lot of time in his room with the door closed and barely made a peep. As I laid in my bed, I couldn't help but feel smug about putting him in his place. It was good that there was a sombre atmosphere in the house, as I was forced to spend a lot more time there than usual. My work shifts had become increasingly sparse and I was basically only used when someone called in sick. So,

I had to conserve my money carefully, meaning that I was confined to my room on most days.

About a week after the fire, the landlord came around to replace the cooker. He hadn't even inspected the damage until that day. All he knew was that there had been a fire and the oven needed replacing. He let himself in and called out to see if anyone was home. No-one else answered his call, so I went down see what he wanted.

I found him standing in the kitchen stroking his slimy beard and inspecting the burnt up cooker. He sneered when he saw me and commented that we had really done a number on that kitchen, and next time perhaps we should consider not cooking while high. I told him that the fire had nothing to do with me, and explained that Guy was the culprit. I said that Guy was careless and a liability to the house. He had left the hob untended, probably because he was drunk or on drugs or something. I told the landlord that the fire had been one of many close calls and that Guy was an accident waiting to happen. The landlord listened to me and changed from stroking his beard to massaging his bald pate, which glistened under the cheap fluorescent glare. I was, of course, angling to get Guy thrown out of the house, but after a prolonged grimace, the landlord just mentioned that he would sort it out in his own way. He then asked me to help him get the new cooker out of his van. However, the "new" cooker was hardly new; it was obviously a second-hand unit and a grubby one at that. It still had grease and grime congealed on it from the previous owner. But, I didn't bother to say anything and just helped him carry it to the kitchen, watching as he connected it up. As he did so, he moaned incessantly about having better things to do on a Friday evening, and that he shouldn't have to be here helping us out. I thought about kicking him square in the back of his bald, bearded head. The money he must make from us and he's complaining about doing one hour of work? What a cunt. Then again, has there ever been a landlord that wasn't a cunt?

When he finished connecting the oven, he stood back and admired his handiwork. I asked him about the burnt worktop. He ran his hand over the charred wood and said that there was nothing he could do to fix it. He pointed to the stretch of worktop on the other side of the hob and said that we could use that part instead. We would just have to live with it the way it was.

I helped him take the burnt cooker to his van and loaded it in the back, all the while listening to him moan about having to go to the dump yard when he could be at home watching TV. I reiterated that it was Guy's fault that he had to waste his Friday like this, but he wasn't listening to me anymore. He was too engrossed in his own self-indulgent whining to comprehend what I was saying. He drove off without thanking me for helping him or even saying goodbye.

Later, when I had returned to my room, I heard some of the housemates coming through the front door. They had obviously been out together. From their voices, I guessed it was Loz, Oscar and Will. They went into the kitchen and I heard them commenting on the replaced cooker. They sounded positive, like it didn't matter that the landlord had given us a second-hand one covered in shit. They were just pleased that it had been replaced.

I decided that they shouldn't let Guy off the hook that easily, so I went downstairs and into the kitchen to stir things up a bit. They appeared shocked at the sight of me voluntarily choosing to be in their presence. I barely greeted them before starting a rant about how we should not be happy with a rank second-hand cooker, and that this was all Guy's fault. I pointed to the charred worktop and told them that the landlord was unwilling to fix it. Thanks to Guy, we now had to make do with a fucked-up kitchen. I said we should all be pissed off with Guy for putting us in this situation through his carelessness. They all just stared at me with dumb expressions on their faces until my rant was over.

Loz retorted that they could just use the bit of the worktop that wasn't burnt, and Will chimed in declaring that a bit of elbow grease would get the cooker looking as good as new - it was no big deal.

But, I wasn't satisfied with that and, just as I was about to launch into another tirade at Guy's expense, he walked through the front door with Pablo in tow behind him. They were both carrying big bags; they had obviously been out doing a lot of shopping.

He came straight into the kitchen and performed a "comical" double take when he saw us all in the kitchen together. Seemingly, his mood had returned to its default setting: obnoxious and enthusiastic.

"Whoa, am I seeing things?" he said on seeing us all gathered in the kitchen. He set the bags down and looked at the newly installed cooker. "Ah, I see. We're all admiring the new and improved cooking unit. Wow, what a beaut. That'll do, indeed!" He ran his hand over the hob and then rubbed his fingers together, trying to wipe the congealed grease off his skin. "Could do with a bit of a clean. But, you lot just leave that to me and Mr Muscle. I'll get this thing looking brand spanking new!" He looked at us all and then averted his gaze, his mood instantly turning rueful. "Look, I just wanted to say that I'm sorry for what I did. There's no excuse for causing that fire. It was negligent and it put everyone in danger. For that, I apologise. I just hope that you can all forgive me and we can start again. Clean slate. Let bygones be bygones. And, just as a way of expressing my apology, me and Pabs here went out shopping and got some things for the house. Some things that we can all use and enjoy."

He dipped into his bags and started revealing the items that he had bought one by one: A six slice toaster, a designer chopping board, a set of stainless steel knives, a George Foreman grill, a water filter, Belgian chocolates, red wine, fancy beers, a bottle of vodka, smoked salmon, a swanky kettle, novelty fridge magnets, and a huge fucking lobster that was still fucking alive. The other housemates swooned and gasped at every item he pulled out of his bag of tricks. It was almost as if they were orgasming at the mere thought of unbridled consumerism.

I stood in the background scowling at what a sly move Guy had pulled off, and at how the others were so easily manipulated with sparkling trinkets. Nothing that he had bought was of any real use. We already had most of those things; they just weren't as new or as shiny, but we still had them nonetheless. I just saw it all as a huge waste. But, Guy had won the house back with his gesture and I knew it.

I slinked out of the kitchen as I couldn't bear the scene anymore, and I swear that as I did so, the lobster fixed its gaze on me with its hollow black eyes, begging me to take it out of that nightmare, to save it from becoming a meal for those insipid prats. I had no choice but to ignore its plea.

The others didn't even notice that I had left the room and as I walked up the stairs, I slumped my shoulders and knew that things had returned to the old ways. Guy was effervescent again and the other housemates were lapping it up.

When I got back into my room, I felt as though the insects on my shelves were laughing at me, mocking my incompetence. They had witnessed all my failures as a human being. They had seen it all and watched me throughout all my pathetic endeavours. Well, they could sit there in their privileged position and judge all they like - it was fucking easy being dead.

A *Tipula paludosa*, or crane fly, was nestled in the corner of the ceiling. I guessed that it was a female as it had a pointed abdomen. It twitched a little, but it seemed perfectly content where it was. She had no desire to search for a mate or go looking for food. She had probably already mated and oviposited her eggs, leaving her with nothing to do except wait for death.

Why did we have to make our human lives so complicated, when in reality our lives are just as simple as that crane fly's? By the next day, she would be curled into a ball and indistinguishable from the dust that surrounded her, completely forgotten. But, all that shit didn't bother her one bit, it only bothers us. The insects on my shelves were all too aware of this, because they were not aware of anything. Nonetheless, I could still feel their eyes boring into me; I looked back into their eyes, which was like staring into an impenetrable void. Their gaze was simply my gaze being returned, and I couldn't bear it.

Based on the noise emanating from downstairs, it was evident that all the joviality had returned. There was laughter, music and games. They were all getting excited about eating that lobster for dinner. That poor lobster, I thought. I imagined myself running downstairs and scooping it out just as it was immersed into the boiling water and then carrying it to freedom, it's joyful pincers clapping in the air like maracas as I ran through the night to set it loose on some salty shore.

But, I would do no such thing. Instead, I merely laid in bed and listened as it screamed from the boiling pot.

That night was long. I couldn't sleep. Their noise kept me awake. In the short time since the fire, I had become accustomed to the peace and quiet, and now it was going to take a bit of time to readjust.

*

Thud-thud. Thud-thud. I woke to a low-level thudding against my wall. It was coming from Guy's room. I couldn't make out what it was, but it sounded like he was repeatedly bouncing a ball up against the wall or kicking it with the back of his heel. The noise was right next to my head, which made it impossible to get back to sleep. I tried to ignore it as much as I could and also tried smothering my head with my pillow to block out the noise. But, it was no use; even if I couldn't hear the noise, I could feel the vibrations reverberating through my mattress, which was just as annoying.

I got out of bed and rubbed my fists into my eyes to wake myself up. The thudding continued. I put my ear up against the wall to see if closer inspection would reveal the cause. But, I couldn't work it out. Thud-thud. Thud-thud. It was merciless in its incessancy. It was starting to get under my skin. Thud-thud. Thud-thud. I looked to the corner of the ceiling to see how the crane fly was doing, but it was gone. I searched the floor around that area and found it curled up dead on the floor. Thud-thud. Thud-thud. Its job had been completed. I scooped it up, opened the window and tipped it out. Thud-thud. Thud-thud. What was that fucking noise? I dressed and washed my face with the water from my hose and then feasted on tinned mackerel in tomato sauce for breakfast. Thud-thud. Thud-thud. What the fuck was Guy doing in there? I couldn't take it anymore, so I went to his room and knocked on his door.

He opened the door and yawned in my face. He was in a dressing gown and his hair was dishevelled, but dishevelled in a way that looked like it was done purposely. He looked at me and squinted. "Oh, good morning, Nil," He said sleepily. "What's the problem? Nothing else is on fire is it?"
I told him that a dull thudding noise was coming from his room and I just wondered what was causing it.
"A dull thudding?" He said. "Well, I've been asleep. I haven't heard any dull thudding. Come in and have a look." I said it was okay, and that I was sorry to bother him. But, he insisted, "No. No. Come in. We can have a look together and get to the bottom of this."
I crossed the threshold and stepped into his room. I peered around and saw that his room starkly contrasted to mine. Firstly, it seemed to be about twice the size of my room. It was spacious, light and smelt of nice things, not like my room, which was cramped, dark and was pungent with sweat and tinned meat. His room was welcoming and had photos of him and his friends on various nights out pinned on a cork board, as well as assorted photos of him travelling and doing various extreme sports: snowboarding, hiking, jumping off a rock face into the sea, skydiving, standing on top of a fucking mountain! Everything was clean and tidy and resembled an advert for Ikea. There was no evidence of anything bubbling under the surface, no trace of any subversive activity. Nevertheless, it was this very cleanliness that rendered it sinister and jarring. In my room, all my perversions were displayed openly, because I was the

only one who was supposed to see them. However, his room was designed to be seen and visited by all, so it was sterile and unassuming. Did he have any perversions at all?

"So where was the noise coming from?" he asked.

I pointed and went over to the part of the room from where I thought the noise was coming from. I searched around and stroked the wall, but for what I didn't know. I could easily see that there was nothing there with just a cursory glance. "Maybe, it was a water pipe or something. They can create quite a noise sometimes," he commented.

I agreed with this explanation and moved in the direction of the door to get the hell out of there. But, as I was walking out, he stopped me.

"That lobster was the fucking tits last night," he said. "Yeah, you should've stuck around and had some. But, you just disappeared." He paused, seemingly in deep thought, then continued. "Because, you know, I wanted to say sorry. For the fire. It was my gift to the house and I wanted you to have something nice to eat."

I told him that it was a nice gesture, but I didn't like lobster.

"Shit. I wish I knew," he replied. "I would have got something else. King prawns, maybe? Steak? Ah, ah, I could've got a joint of lamb braised in mint!" He paused again; I think he was waiting for me to indicate my preference. I didn't though. I just stayed silent, so he continued with his spiel regardless. "A nice bit of lamb. Yes, that would've been sweet! Well, savoury, but you know what I mean!" Pause. "Because, I wanted to apologise, because of the fire."

I told him not to worry about the fire. It was no big deal after all.

"Well, that's not the message I got from the landlord," he quickly retorted. "Someone was not happy at all. The feeling I got from the landlord was that someone in the house was very upset about me. Thinks I've been causing all sorts of problems. Maybe that person is someone who is threatened by others enjoying themselves. Maybe that someone just can't bear to see others having a good time and getting on with each other. Maybe that someone needs to lighten up and live life rather than constantly fight against it?" Even though Guy's message was seemingly one of outright resentment towards me, he said it all in such a light-hearted and jolly manner that I honestly couldn't tell whether he was berating me or trying to lift my spirits in a sincere attempt to make me change my miserable ways. It was such a masterful piece of delivery that I felt belittled, and yet still unthreatened in his presence.

I just stood there, looked as nonchalant as I could and told him that I didn't know who that person could be. Maybe Loz?

"There's no point in dwelling on it," he said. "What's done is done. I just think that person would be happier if he joined in and saw that inclusion is healthy and rewarding."

I said that he was probably right, and thanked him for letting me check his room for the noise. As I began to walk out of his room, he called me back. "Just one more thing," he said. "I don't know if you've heard, but Pablo sadly has to return to Spain immediately for family reasons. So, unfortunately, we are going to lose one of our good friends in the house. It's sad I know, but to send him off in style, we are going to throw him a huge party in the house tonight. You don't have any problems with that, do you?"

I said I would prefer it if there wasn't a party in the house because of the noise.

He said, "Well, you'll obviously be coming to the party, as I'm sure you don't want to miss Pablo's send off. So, the noise won't be a problem."

I said that I still would rather there wasn't a party in the house.

"Everyone has been invited now, so it's too late to change it. But, I'll remember your preference for the next time. You can also invite anyone you want. I'm sure you've got loads of friends that would enjoy a party."

I told him I would see what they're doing.

"Good! Gonna be a mental night. Dancing, music, drinking. The whole shebang! You'll have a great time. I'll make sure of it."

I walked back to my room fantasising about throttling Guy with my bare hands. As soon as I was in my room, I picked up my phone and called the landlord. When he answered, I told him all about the party and that loads of people had been invited. My thinking was that he would come round and put a stop to the festivities. But instead, he growled and said that he wasn't our mother and he couldn't give a shit what we did. He said that he had better things to do with his Saturday than to deal with our little spats. He hung up without saying goodbye and I called him a cunt into the phone, even though I knew he was no longer listening. Then, out of nowhere, the thudding noise started up again. Thud-thud. Thud-thud. Was it a water pipe? Was it my heartbeat? Was it a voice inside my head? I closed my eyes and listened intently. It seemed as though the beats were a message: Thud-thud. Thud-thud. En-joy. En-joy. En-joy. Thud-thud.

Fuck you! I shouted at the noise, grabbed my jacket and decided to go out for a long and aimless walk.

*

When I returned from the walk, the preparations for the party were already under way. Guy was assembling large cubes of marinated lamb and chicken on barbecue skewers. Pablo was setting up a makeshift DJ table in the kitchen with his laptop connected through an amp and large speakers positioned on either side of the table. Will was tearing open bags of ice and filling up an empty dustbin, which I guessed would be used as some sort of cooling receptacle for the stacks of cheap Polish beer that was blocking the entrance to the kitchen.

I tried to slink past unnoticed, but it was no use, Guy clocked me almost instantly. "Yo, Nil!" he shouted, "We've been waiting for you. Come on, get in here and help us get ready. There's a lot of work to do before the party and there's not much time until people start arriving."

I said that it was still only eleven in the morning and that there should be plenty of time before it started.

"Nah, bro. It's an all-dayer. People are gonna come at around two or three. Gonna have a nice BBQ and some beer and listen to some chilled out reggae. Then, as the night grows, so will we, man! Up the ante and start throwing some shapes. This party is NEVER gonna end!"

I climbed over the stacks of beer and listlessly entered the kitchen. I had resigned myself to the fact that I would just have to tolerate this bullshit party and get through it the best I could. I asked Guy how we could possibly have a barbecue when the garden was in such a state.

"Yeah, tell me about it. That garden is a jungle. That's why Loz and Oscar are on that detail. They are out there now just fucking Titmarshing the shit out of it. We need you out there now, to help them out. It's a glorious day out there, so go out and enjoy it. Summer is now truly here, boy!"

I made for the back door.

"Oh yeah," he said. "Just to let you know we had to disconnect your hose system as we needed the outside tap, and also, because you know, it looked a bit weird. Hope you don't mind."

I said that it was fine, but really I was picturing myself taking one of those skewers he was using and jabbing it straight through his eye and through the back of his thick skull, and then having a Guy-brained kebab. Now that would be the sweetest of all barbecues.

Outside in the garden, Loz and Oscar had already done much of the work. It was a small garden so even though it was overgrown and wild, there was not much square meterage and the task was not as arduous as it might have initially seemed. They had uprooted most of the weeds and had revealed what lay beneath the vegetation. We could now see that the garden was mostly paving slabs, but with a thin strip of soil around the outside that framed the hard centre. The strip of soil was probably once used for flowers, but, over time, the weeds had won the race for life and had mercilessly hogged all the sunlight and nutrients, leaving the flowers for dust. I wondered about all the hundreds of thousands of insects that had made that wild garden their home and how many had now been lost in this brutal purge sanctioned by the ruthless Guy in his quest for enjoyment. It's a hard world for the little things, I concluded.

Loz welcomed me onto the gardening team and then apologised for disconnecting my hoses. The hoses were neatly rolled up in the corner of the garden. I wondered how they had managed to get the other sides of the hoses out of my room. Did they go to my room and release them, or did they yank them out of the window from down below in the garden? Each of those scenarios angered me, as they were both equally thoughtless. But, I swallowed the bile and set about helping them finish clearing up the garden, which basically just involved ripping out the weeds and throwing them over the back fence into the communal alleyway located behind. There was no consideration for the other surrounding residents. What if they needed to use that alleyway? That didn't seem to bother Loz or Oscar. Nothing was going to get in the way of their party.

I couldn't count how many times they commented on the weather while they were working outside. They were obsessed with azure skies and baking sunshine. I found that weather to be fucking annoying. I was sweating and uncomfortable. My clothes itched and stuck to my body. I was becoming agitated due to the burning sensation on my skin and on the top of my head, and the glare from the sunlight was hurting my eyes. It felt as though I was being cooked in an oven. I didn't understand what people found so appealing about that kind of weather. Was it something innate that humans were born with or was it because we have been taught our whole lives to perceive such conditions as enjoyable? To me, the most practical and agreeable weather was completely overcast and about 20 degrees Celsius. Weather that was neutral and functional, not only for carrying out your day-to-day tasks, but also for working, driving, sitting around the house and for choosing your clothes to wear that day. But, fucking sunshine, I fucking hated it.

Guy came out to see how we were getting on with the job. He was the tacit boss who was checking on his workers, who were not reimbursed financially, but bribed with the promise of a better time, a more fulfilling experience.

"Man, I'd love to be working out here with you lot. Just soak in this weather. Drink it down. This is glorious." Guy said as he spread his arms out and turned his head up to the sky like fucking Jesus.

Loz and Oscar, of course, agreed sycophantically with everything he said and gazed piously at their new saviour as he just continued to bask in the rays showering down on his face.

"There's just something about this weather," he mused. "Something that just hits you deep inside and makes like this glow in your stomach, which then just radiates through every cell in your body and makes you happy. Sunshine just makes everything better, makes a miserable day a great day, makes a chore into a pleasant activity, makes a dour and uninspiring place seem vivid and wonderful and welcoming. When the weather's like this, I just want to be outside all the time. I don't care where, I'll find a piece of grass in the middle of a goddamn highway roundabout and sit there. All's good in the world when the sun is shining upon it."

Loz and Oscar were hanging onto his every word, the messiah was sermonising and they were just lapping it up.

"Reminds me of my time travelling when I stayed on the beaches of Gili Air in Indonesia. Just chillin' and learning how to dive. That's where I became a dive master. Just sinking in that cool clear water every day and checking out what Mother Nature was hiding under the sea. What an experience that was. I'll cherish my time there forever and how it made me realise how we must respect the earth and the sea. Only through experience can we see it for ourselves, how important nature and ecology are. Everyone should go travelling, man. Broadens your mind, expands your soul, opens your heart to this world. This fragile world."

I looked around at the decimated garden and wondered how that was compatible with his ecological philosophy. However, Loz and Oscar were in a state of reverie, dreaming of distant exotic lands where they could fucking bum around and pretend they were learning something about the world. I just felt sick from hearing such utter shit.

I couldn't bear it any longer, so I picked up my hoses and excused myself, saying that I was going to put them back in my room. Guy dropped his Jesus-on-the-cross pose and pointed his finger at me. "Don't be gone too long, boyo," he said. "I don't want you missing out on this magnificent sunshine. Vitamin D all round!"

I nodded at him and hurried into the house, just thankful to get out of that oppressive heat for a while.

When I got into my room, I took some time to rest and sat on my bed. I looked at my insect collection and then thought again of all the insects that had either died or been disturbed purely as a result of this party.

"Nil!" I heard Guy scream from the garden. "Nil, we have a beer waiting for you, bro! Come and get it while it's cold!"

I sighed the deepest sigh that's ever been sighed and trudged down the stairs and out to the back garden.

All of the housemates were in the garden drinking beer, basking in the sunshine. Guy approached me and handed over a can. I reluctantly cracked it open and took a tiny, laboured sip, wincing at the taste.

Guy took a look around the garden. "You boys have done an outstanding job on this garden! Looks like something out of Ideal Home magazine. We are all ready for the party! Nothing can stand in our way now. Cheers!"

Guy raised his can of beer and we all felt obliged to pointlessly tap our beer cans together. I thought about how I preferred the garden when it was wild and pest-ridden. Goodbye, my tiny friends, you are fallen but not forgotten.

"Man, this party is going to kick serious arse!" Guy growled with a battle cry. The others growled in response.

I edged back and watched them all growling together like apes. Maybe this garden was still wild after all, I thought.

*

By the time the first guest had arrived, the house had been cleaned, the dustbin was overflowing with ice and beer, the garden had been shorn bare, the DJ equipment was rigged up, the food prepared, and the barbecue lit.

I watched through the kitchen window as Guy was using a stick to shuffle coals around the barbecue in the garden; he was trying to get the heat to spread from one coal to the other. What a twat. It was clear that he really liked to be in charge, and that kind of self-given authority was something that really got under my skin. He had no reason to assume that role or for others to accept that he was taking it - but everyone just blindly went along with it, like he had some God-given right to be the leader. I think the fact that he truly believed in this self-made position with no appearance of self-doubt is what cemented this position in the group.

I watched as Guy welcomed each guest that arrived with excessive jubilation. He treated every person who came through that door and into the party like they were the single most important person in the room. "Great to see you!!" he would shout. "So glad you could make it! Come on in!". It was all posturing. He even did it to people he hardly knew or had never seen before. To me, it looked insincere, but the guests seemed to instantly warm to his overbearing hospitality.

Soon, the number of people at the party had swelled to around twenty. They were all crammed into the tiny back garden engaged in pointless activities like jostling for sunlight, crawling over each other for beer and cubes of charred meat, laughing at their own jokes and chattering incessantly about nothing.

More people turned up, which meant that Guy overcooked more meat and everyone drank more beer. The chattering grew louder and more aggressive in tone and they all continued to jostle and fight for space and conversation.

And, still more came.

The incessant din from the chattering became even louder and I began to suspect that all the laughter I heard at that party was forced and insincere. The conversations appeared strained and frustrating. Was anyone really having a good time?

Even more people arrived.

And, even more beer flowed. The music changed; it became louder and more aggressive, reflecting the alcohol-soaked mood.

The males began to pluck up the courage to gain the females' attention. They performed and danced and pretended they were having the time of their lives in order to make an impression. The females were either impressed or completely unimpressed; I couldn't tell - their countenance unreadable.

The barbecue ended and the leftover meat became cold and gristly. But that didn't stop the guests cramming it into their salivating jaws and feasting on the fat and grease.

More people arrived.

More alcohol.

Louder.

Dancing.

Enjoyment or anger? I couldn't decide what these people were feeling.

I couldn't understand what I was seeing. I didn't understand what any of them were doing or what they were talking about. I just didn't understand…

I then had what I can only describe as an out-of-body experience, or to put it more accurately, an inner-body experience. A feeling where I became only my body and nothing else. Where the world of the conscious served no meaning or order, where nothing was understood. Where the word "understood" was non-existent, as there were no words or things to understand. There were no feelings; there was just a void. This void contained falling, twisting shapes and sounds of a world I could not comprehend; a language that was shattered into fragments until it was just white noise in my brain - a state of utter meaningless. It was a feeling that is impossible to put into words, as the words themselves do not exist to explain such a sensation. It was a world without words. It was a world plunged into an abyss. I was a foreign body in an alien world.

I don't know how long that feeling lasted, because time did not exist there either, and I only snapped out of that trance-like state because of the sound of Guy's booming and clear voice. He had began ranting to a group of drunken revellers. His voice was the only thing capable of cutting through all the noise and confusion.

"Maaaaaan!" he said. "I feel so at one! The people. I just... I just love the people here. All the people. I feel so at one with you all. It's amazing to have you all here. The drinking. The dancing. The music! Oh, especially the music! You know that feeling when you listen to a song and it just hits you? It just hits you right here, in the pit of your stomach. In a place so deep, and so emotional. And you don't even know why it hits you there. It's like you're connected to something else, something larger than us, something beyond the realms of explanation.

The hairs on your arms stand on end and everything just seems to make perfect sense. Have you ever felt that before? When you listen to a song and everything just makes sense, and you feel connected? How does music have the power to do that? That's the power of it. Art at its purest!"

I listened to the music to see what he was talking about, but to me, it just sounded like a repetitive beat with the same chords, lyrics and structure as all the other thousands of songs - a bland three-minute bludgeoning of the eardrums.

The others all agreed with Guy, and all appeared to feel the same way about music. What were they hearing that I wasn't? What was this feeling of connection or this deep place in your stomach it was supposed to hit?

As the song faded out, Guy raised his arms and shouted to everyone in the vicinity, "Right, everyone! For this next song, I want you all to dance like no one's watching!" Everyone cheered in response and proceeded to dance in a maniacal and wild fashion to the next song that played.

I couldn't bear to be at that party anymore. I don't even know how or why I had tolerated it for as long as I did; maybe just out of some morbid curiosity.

I grabbed a handful of peanuts, headed for the front door and decided to go for another one of my long and pointless walks. I needed to clear my head. I needed to be alone.

*

I walked around the neighbouring streets for a while, but that didn't eat up anywhere near enough time, so I spontaneously decided to get the Underground and see where that took me.

The Tube reeked of sweat, piss and farts, and was full of drunken revellers, all spouting drunken bullshit. I wondered if they realised how loud and obnoxious they actually were, or if they even cared. A band of gipsy musicians boarded and began playing some sort of accordion music. A group of young girls who were listening and dancing to music from their phones stopped what they were doing and laughed at the gipsy band's song, probably because it wasn't cool enough for them. Personally, I thought the accordion song was equally as cheap and tacky as the dance tracks they were playing. I didn't understand why they would choose one style of music over another; deem one to be acceptable and the other a joke. The choice seemed arbitrary to me. I wondered what might have been if society had in fact deemed downbeat stoicism to be a worthy trait - I might have finally fit in.

After the gipsy band finished their music, they walked through the carriage with an empty coffee cup, gesturing for people to give them money. Everyone ignored them as if they were invisible. I felt a brief moment of pity for them and almost reached into my pocket to hand over some change, but I didn't. Instead, when they walked up to me, I ignored them just like the rest of the passengers had done.

The train began to fill up and I was pushed up against the doors. Subsequently, I was forced off at Covent Garden by the mob of people disembarking, then swept out of the station exit before I even knew what had happened.

The night was wild with people singing and laughing, many spilling out from the pubs and onto the streets drinking pints of beer and smoking. There were street performers everywhere plying their trade to families and general onlookers. Everyone was delighted with the performances they were watching, and were clapping and smiling widely. I couldn't believe they were watching the same thing as I was. From where I was standing, the performances were utter bilge. Maybe the people were just happy to be getting something for free?

I walked further and watched couples and groups of friends sitting in restaurants eating and chatting. I couldn't understand why anyone would go out to eat just for fun. Maybe I could understand if it was because you were too lazy to cook your own meal, or out of necessity if you didn't have access to your own cooking apparatus. But, for fun? And, even stranger than that, I saw people taking photos of their food before shoving it down their gullets. I wondered if they also took photos of it the next day when it had transformed into hardened black shit at the bottom of a toilet bowl. I realised that I was living in a world full of smug, self-absorbed arseholes. All they cared about was personal enjoyment, as if it was a selectable photographic filter on their phone. If something wasn't made explicitly or implicitly enjoyable, then it served no purpose. The question for me was why I personally didn't feel this kind of enjoyment? Why did I have no propensity to dine out for a meal, to seek out new foods, to drink alcohol, to mingle and socialise, to listen to music, to watch a film or be told a story, to bask in sunlight, to mutilate my body with tattoos or piercings, or to fucking dance like no one's watching? My only desires were to eat when hungry, drink when thirsty, sleep when tired and find appropriate shelter. Was I really an insect trapped in a human body? It certainly felt that way. Humans seemed stranger to me than any other creature I had encountered; a species so alien to the world around it that it would seek to distort it at any cost to make it more palatable to its alien mind. For a species that deemed itself to be highly intelligent, it sure had a hard time making peace with the world in which it was conceived. Forever at odds with it; forever trying to mutilate or destroy it in some way.

To others, I seemed to be the one who was on the outside; a person who could not connect or fit in. I was the outcast. However, from my perspective, I was the only one who fit in with this world perfectly. I accepted it for what it was, in all its dispassionate emptiness. To me, it was the other people who were the outcasts, who could never accept the innate emptiness that surrounded them.

I couldn't stand walking around that place anymore, so I decided to head back. It was around twelve o clock, so I thought that Guy's party must have been coming to an end.

When I got back to the station, it was even more packed with people than before. Everyone was scrambling to get back home after their night out and were drunk and aggressive. They stank and slurred their words, swaying to and fro with no awareness of what was happening around them.

I made it to the platform and waited in the crowd for the Tube to arrive. Everyone was vying for space at the front of the platform to make sure they were able to board the next train. I was being jostled from side to side as if I wasn't there. A group of men behind me started screaming out a football song about their team being the greatest. The noise blasted my eardrums. Then, with seemingly no regard for the other people on the platform, they jumped up and down and swung their arms about to celebrate their team's victory over another team. They did realise that they had had absolutely no involvement in that win, didn't they? Obviously not by the way they were celebrating.

The Tube arrived and there was a mad rush to get on. It was already half full, so it was a struggle. However, everyone somehow found a way. We became a pile of flesh. People were sticking to each other, bodily odours mixing together creating a rancid stench, hair getting tangled in each other's mouths. We became a single entity: a disgusting mass of amalgamated flesh, bone, hair and clothing fabrics. The heat was unbearable and sweat poured from our foreheads, which added a twist of salt to the thick soup of human particles that already permeated the air. I felt as though I was on the verge of a panic attack, and hoped that at the next stop, the crowd would thin out a bit. But, instead, even more people forced their way on, expanding the human entity. An armpit smothered my face, its sweat blended with the sweat from my forehead. A drop fell and stung my upper lip and I couldn't move my hand to wipe it off, so it sat there on the precipice of my mouth, waiting to enter and be consumed. Someone stood on my foot with a piercing stiletto and clamped it to the floor. I tried to wriggle my foot from under the vice-like heel, but again, there was nowhere for my foot to move.

I closed my eyes and thought about any place other than that meat grinder of a train in which I found myself. I thought of acres of grassy plains, deserted snow-blanketed shores, vast deserts of sand and nothing else. But, none of those images worked; none of them were serene enough. But then, an image came to me, a blissful and calming image - it was an image of a house free from other housemates. A house all to myself, away from everyone. Empty room after empty room, peaceful and silent. No-one to answer to, no-one to have to avoid. Just an empty house, with only me in it. I clung onto this perfect image until I was jarred out of my reverie at the next station by the train jerking to an abrupt halt.

There was another mad rush of people getting off, who were quickly replaced by those getting on. Now, the only image I could see was a termite colony. Thousands upon thousands of pests crawling over each other.

However, at least termites worked together for the greater good, I thought. I had no idea what the humans on this Tube were working towards.

By the time the train had reached my stop, the mass of flesh had thinned out. I exited the Underground station and trudged back to the house, hoping, hoping that by the time I got there, the party had ended, or at least coming to a close. But, I had no idea how far off the mark I actually was.

*

If anything, by the time I arrived home, the party was just kicking off. As soon as I walked through the door, I was struck by the combined smell of marijuana smoke, vomit and beer. Excruciatingly dull and repetitive dance music filled the air and it was a struggle to make it to the other end of the hall having to navigate through all the oblivious party guests. There were at least twice as many people there than before, and more were arriving. Everyone was drunk, just like the people I had seen on the streets and the Tube. Nevertheless, these guests somehow appeared louder and even more obnoxious.

I just wanted get to my room, close the door, and shut out all those drunken morons. But, as I struggled through the hall, Pablo noticed me and grabbed me by the arm. He was drunk out of his mind and his breath smelt of animal shit. He mumbled some incomprehensible nonsense and dragged me into the kitchen where the DJ was blasting out his monotonous dance music. Pablo began shouting something to me, trying to get his voice heard over the music. I couldn't completely understand what he was talking about, but I think he was saying that he was extremely sad to be leaving, and that he had had one of the best times of his life in the house, and that it had been such an amazing and fulfilling experience. I rolled my eyes and stopped listening to him. I just watched his disgusting lips twist and bend as spit sprayed continuously out of his mouth as he spouted his bullshit.

Thankfully, his attention was soon diverted when he saw Loz and Oscar come in from the garden - they were just as intoxicated as Pablo was. He called them over, and they all cheered and held up their cans of beer. Loz then went back over to the kitchen window and banged on it, gesturing for Guy and Will to come in too.

Soon, all the housemates were clustered together in the kitchen sharing a drunken embrace. Guy tried to pull me into the group hug, but I stood rigidly, attempting to resist getting drawn in. He was much stronger than me though, so when he tried a second time, I was easily dragged into their stinking, moist arms.

"It's been great being your friend, Pablo, my man!" Guy shouted as he forcibly held me in their embrace. "We're just all so sad to see you go, it won't be the same without you. I hope we managed to at least give you a good send-off with this little party?"

Pablo was so emotionally affected by Guy's words that tears started streaming down his face and he hugged even harder, which made Guy's grip loosen, giving me the chance to slip free.

I pulled out of the hug and edged back towards the kitchen door. They were all so drunk that they didn't notice that I had wriggled free. Well, no one noticed except for Guy, who was tracking me out of the corner of his eye the whole time. I stood at the kitchen door and looked back at them ensconced in their bizarre group cuddle. Guy, still tracking me, frowned menacingly in my direction. I could tell he was not pleased with my withdrawal from the group bonding session. I was unnerved by his sinister gaze. He could not work out what my motivations were and what I wanted from life, and this angered or even frightened him.

I backed out of the kitchen door and climbed the stairs, the vision of Guy's dark stare carved into my mind. All I wanted now was to go to bed and get away from everyone. But, the upstairs areas were also filled with guests partying, drinking, talking and hanging out in the bedrooms.

A male and a female guest were passionately kissing each other up against the door to my room. I tried asking them to move out of the way, but they either ignored me or were oblivious to my protestations. After a few attempts at trying to get their attention vocally, I finally gave up on the niceties and forcefully pushed them out of the way. They slid off my door and fell onto the floor, still engaged in their passionate kiss. I unlocked the door to my room and slipped in, while the couple, unconcerned by my presence, continued their lurid display rolling around on the floor outside my room.

Once inside, I locked my door, flopped on my bed and wrapped a pillow around my head.

The noise in my bedroom was immense and the vibrating thudding from the music downstairs pounded through the walls. THUD-THUD. THUD-THUD. THUD-THUD. THUD-THUD. It was the same tempo and tone as the thudding noise that had been coming from Guy's room that very morning, only amplified a hundred times. I laid in bed and listened to the cheers, jeers and laughter, the shrill screams of anger and argument, the thumping feet and kicking walls and falling over, furniture being knocked about and the drunken singing and shouting of song lyrics out of tune and out of time. It was clear that I would not be granted a single second of sleep that night. I thought back to the garden and how peaceful it was when it was only the inhabited by insects. Now, it was overrun with humans all desperate for personal gratification. The noise of EN-JOY EN-JOY EN-JOY EN-JOY.

*

The music must have stopped at about five in the morning, and I fell asleep soon after that.

When I awoke around four or five hours later, I pushed my ear up to my door to see if I could hear any noise from the house, but it was silent. I hoped that everyone had finally gone, but when I opened my door, I saw that the man and woman I had pushed over the previous night were still on the floor where I had left them. They were now half-naked in a spooning position, sleeping soundly.

The doors to the other bedrooms were all open and they contained guests sprawled out asleep on the floors and the beds. I needed to take a piss so I edged open the bathroom door, but stopped halfway as the smell wafting out was too much to bear. I pinched my nose and peered around the door - there was puke all over the sink and the floor. Also, the toilet must have somehow been blocked as it was now overflowing with shit and toilet paper. There were also piles of shit in the bathtub, probably as that was the only place to go after the toilet had started overflowing. I decided to just hold in my piss and I made my way downstairs. More guests were asleep in the other two downstairs bedrooms. The kitchen was badly hit too. Beer cans, cigarette butts, puke and greasy discarded foods were everywhere. The garden had obviously been used as an outdoor urinal all night. The late morning air was pungent with the odour of piss and burnt out coal. I couldn't believe the level of disrespect everyone had shown for the house.

I decided that I just needed to get out of there; I needed to find a cheap coffee shop in which to sit, so I could use their toilet, have some water and also stay out of the house for enough time to let the others clear up the mess. I crept towards the front door, but just before I was about to leave, I heard a voice coming from behind me.

"Where are you going, bro?" it said.

I turned around and saw that it was Guy. He was standing in the doorway of the kitchen. He was still in the same clothes that he had been wearing the previous night, but he didn't look as hungover or as dishevelled as the others who were sprawled about the place.

I told him that I was just popping out to get something to eat.

"Yeah, I understand that," he said "but can't it wait until we give this place a clean-up?"

I told him that the mess wasn't really anything to do with me, and I wasn't sure why I should be responsible for clearing it up.

"What, you think that all of this mess is mine?!" he said. I detected agitation in his voice. "All this is not mine, but I'm still going to clear it up. Because that's what you do after a party. You all chip in to help clean up the mess."

I started to become angry myself, so through gritted teeth, I mentioned that I was barely present during the party, so it really had nothing to do with me.

He shook his head and said, "I clearly remember you being there and enjoying the beer and the barbecue and getting involved in our farewell hug for Pablo. Yes, you were at the party all right. You had a great time, and now you want to bail on the cleaning duties? That's not cool, man."

I said I didn't care if he saw me at the party or not. I wasn't there for long and didn't want the party in the house in first place and he knew it. I said that I was going out and expected the place to be clean when I returned.

"You go then. That's cool. We'll use your room as a resting room for the guests that are too hungover to leave. Some of them are pretty pukey, so I hope you have clean bed sheets waiting because you'll be needing to change them when you get back."

But, I told him that I had locked my door so there was no way anyone could get in.

"Oh, didn't you know?" he replied smugly. "These locks are cheap as chips, matey. All our keys work on each other's doors, well, if you jiggle them enough. You can get into anyone's room if you have the right technique. How do you think we got into your room to disconnect those hoses? Well, anyway, you go and we can just let people into your room by ourselves. You have a good time then!" And with that, he disappeared back into the kitchen.

I knew I couldn't leave now. There was no way I could stomach people going into my room and sleeping on my bed. The thought of it made me nauseous. I had no choice but to stay and help clear up all the mess. Firstly, I went into the garden and took a long piss up the wall. There were countless other piss stains all up the same wall, so I thought another one wouldn't make a difference.

I then went back to Guy and told him that I had considered what he had said and decided that helping out was the right thing to do.

"I knew you would come round. You're a good dude, Nil," he said, giving me a bin bag to start collecting all the detritus that was strewn over the floor.

One by one, the guests started waking up in their zombified states and began leaving the house, not one of them offering to help us with the cleaning. They shuffled out of the door like the previous night was one big embarrassing mistake, and perhaps it was.

Loz, Will and Oscar all eventually woke up. They stared at the mess like someone had just committed genocide and they were the ones tasked with cleaning up the bodies. Pablo was still out cold so Guy suggested we let him stay asleep; it was a party for him after all. We moved the few remaining guests who were still too hungover or lazy to leave into Loz's room and we pulled straws on who would get what detail to clean up.

The longest was the straw for the kitchen, the second longest for the garden, the third for the upstairs bedrooms, the fourth for the downstairs bedrooms and communal areas, and lastly, the shortest one was for bathroom detail. I prayed that I would not get bathroom detail - anything but that.

We all picked the straws from Guy's hand and then laid them on the table to see our fate. FUCK. I, of course, drew the shortest straw. I caught Guy smirking at this, which made me wonder whether he had set the whole thing up in the first place - my punishment for not conforming to his rules.

I found some old rubber gloves in the cupboard, cobbled together as many cleaning utensils as I could and made my way upstairs. I didn't think that any day could be worse than the previous one, but as I opened the door to the bathroom, I realised how wrong I was.

I was witness to the inevitable outcome of human enjoyment; all that fancy food that I saw the people taking photos of in the restaurants last night, the barbecue with the marinated meats, the beer, the drugs, and the dancing all led to one thing: excrement. And, here it was packed into this room, the consequences of all our actions and purchases. Everything processed into brown, disgusting, useless, stinking shit. Unfortunately, I was the one that had been chosen to get rid of it, to rid their collective conscience of this embarrassing by-product of their excess, to flush it away, to dispel it into another reality - a reality that they were not willing to confront themselves.

We are all shit and everything we do is shit and everything will all ultimately end up as shit.

I repeated this mantra in my head as I scooped the shit out of the bathtub and bagged it up. I repeated it again as I jammed the plunger into the toilet and pumped away to try and unblock the soil pipe. I repeated it while faecal matter splattered back into my face as I worked the plunger up and down. I repeated it as I cleaned all the shit from the room. I became less and less bothered about being hit by shit; the more I was covered in it, the less it mattered.

WE ARE ALL SHIT AND EVERYTHING WE DO IS SHIT AND EVERYTHING WILL ALL ULTIMATELY END UP AS SHIT.

After I finished the chore, I took the longest shower I've ever had and scrubbed my body a countless number of times. I think I also cried.

After I was done, I went to my room. I didn't want to see or talk to the rest of the housemates.

Later, I heard the others say their last goodbyes to Pablo as he left to go to back to Spain. I hoped his little party was worth it, the cunt.

*

I felt so demeaned by the toilet cleaning episode that I locked myself in my room for a few days and didn't emerge again until I couldn't bear being cooped up any longer. I waited for an opening when all the other tenants had gone out and ventured downstairs into the kitchen.

The house was back to normal; the party was now just a memory and even the garden had begun to sprout weeds again.

I took a glass off the draining board and began to pour myself some water from the tap. But, before the glass was half full, I heard the front door swing open. I downed the water from the glass in one gulp and cursed at the house for never allowing me a second of peace. I assumed that it would be Guy coming home, so I threw the glass into the sink and tried to get back up to my room before he had a chance to talk to me.

When I came out of the kitchen, I saw that it wasn't Guy, or any of the other housemates for that matter, but a young woman who was struggling through the doorway with her luggage and possessions.

She looked up at me and I stared back. Usually, I would have done everything possible to avoid this situation, but I was mesmerised.

She wore no makeup and had simple long jet-black hair; she was dressed in basic jeans and a grey T-shirt. Maybe some would call her plain, but I found her irresistible. And, here it was. The one thing that I felt connected me to other humans: a sexual appetite. We at least shared that, annoying and pointless as it was. It was definitely something that I didn't want and tried my best to suppress, as it was pointless for someone like me to have sexual desires. I had realised long ago that I wasn't the type of person that could ever attract a mate. For the most part, it never even come up as I was rarely in the position where I was around women. But, during the rare times that I was, I would try my best to ignore their presence by staring at the floor or acting aloof. I had never been engaged in any sexual experience of any kind, not even a feel of a breast or a kiss on the lips. I guessed that this was pretty strange. But, I suppose to others, I *was* pretty strange.

I welcomed her to the house and introduced myself. She loosely shook my hand and told me her name was Jana. She seemed disinterested, but I continued to pry. I asked her where she was from and she said Estonia. How long have you been here? A couple of months. Where were you living in London before? Not far from here.

Her answers were concise and I sensed she just wanted to get to her room. She said that the landlord had given her a key and that's all she knew about the place. I told her that I knew which room was hers and helped her carry her possessions. She thanked me and closed the door to her room in my face. I really liked her.

I went back to the kitchen and made some breakfast. I remained in the kitchen for a while in the vain hope that she might come down and want to have a conversation. I couldn't believe it - I actually wanted to engage in conversational small talk. Annoyingly, she never made an appearance, so I went back to my room and did some research on the *Aphis lantanae* in order to clear my mind.

Later, the other housemates came home and Guy somehow sensed that someone new had moved in. I heard him knocking on her door and greeting her in his ostentatious manner. I listened carefully to see how she would react, but I didn't hear anything from her part. Then, Guy asked her what she was doing that night, and said that it was a tradition in the house that all new housemates were taken to the pub so they could get to know everyone. She told him that she was very tired and was just going to have a night in.

Guy, unsure how to respond to her cold attitude, said that he understood and that they would do it another night instead. She didn't respond and just shut the door on him. I punched the air victoriously. Take that, Guy! There's two of us now, your grip on this house is loosening, I thought.

I wanted to go to her room and thank her for not falling for Guy's insidious ways, but I refrained, realising how creepy that might seem. Instead, I waited until the following day when I heard someone rustling around in the kitchen and then made my way down hoping that it would be her. Unfortunately, it wasn't - it was Guy. I tried to sneak back upstairs without him noticing, but he instantly clocked me.

"Hey, Nil. What brings you to the sacred kingdom of the kitchen?" he said.

I told him I was just coming to make a cup of tea and put the kettle on.

"Kettle in your room broken then?"

I said I just needed to get out of my room for a bit.

"Well, you're always welcome in the kitchen, you know that. Even if your visits are rare," he quipped. "Look, I just wanted to say thank you for cleaning the bathroom after the party the other day. It must've been a tough job and we didn't get to thank you for it. I'm sure Pablo would have wanted to thank you for it too, but you weren't there when we saw him off."

I told Guy that it was because I was feeling extremely ill after having to clean that bathroom. I said that I must have been contaminated after being exposed to so much faecal matter.

"Those are the breaks, I guess," Guy shrugged. Then, he quickly changed the subject, "Hey, so have you seen the new housemate at all? It's a girl, you know"

I told him I had briefly met her, but we didn't speak much.

"Seems like quite a shy one," he mused. "I have to find a way to get her out of her shell. It's not healthy to be cooped up in your room all day and night without socialising..." he looked me straight in the eyes, "...that kind of behaviour is just... weird."

I poured the boiled water into my mug and then started for the kitchen door.

"Going back to your room?" Guy said snidely.

I didn't reply and took the tea back to my room, waiting for another possible opportunity to talk to Jana.

That night, I again heard that thudding noise coming from Guy's room. It kept me awake for ages. Was it the pipes? Or could it really be Guy purposely making the noise to frazzle me into submission? Was he that insane? I comforted myself with thoughts of Jana and what she might be doing in her room. If I could just get her on my side, then we could bring down Guy together. She was just like me; even though I had only talked to her for less than five minutes, I knew she was just like me. We were the same. I knew it. Thud-thud. Thud-thud.

*

I finally managed to "bump into" her a couple of days later. I heard rustling in the kitchen again, and I knew all the others were out together as I had overheard them talking earlier about going to the park to have a "kick about". I rushed downstairs to catch her before she left and found her putting away some food that she had just bought from the supermarket. I checked the items she was removing from her shopping bag - they were dry rice cakes. That was my kind of food: long-lasting and functional. No-one was going to throw a dinner party and serve rice cakes and no-one was ever going to take a photo of a rice cake and post it on the internet. So, rice cakes were fine by me.

I asked her how she was coping in the house, she shrugged and said that it was fine for a cheap place to live. I asked her why she was in London. She said, "university". I asked her what she thought of the area. She said it was alright, but she couldn't find anywhere to buy cheap furniture for her room. This was where I seized the opportunity to wrangle my way in. I told her that I knew of a place and that I could take her there if she liked. She looked at me blankly, then pursed her lips considering my offer. After a moment of contemplation, she thanked me and asked me when I could take her. I said that now was a good time. She said okay, and that was that. She quickly stored the rest of her shopping and we departed to go to the outlet store that I had found when buying items for my room.

The store was a bus ride away and we largely sat in silence during the journey. She only talked when absolutely necessary. She seemed to be completely comfortable with silence; there was no fiddling of the fingers or desperately thinking of something to discuss. When there was nothing to say, she just stared out of the window and looked at the world passing by as if it was no concern to her if it was all just suddenly sucked into a vortex and disappeared forever.

I wanted to determine whether under her cold exterior she was like the others or like me, so I asked her what she liked doing. She said that she was here to study. I asked her what she did for fun. She stared out of the window and didn't respond. I asked again and made a few suggestions. Clubs? Music? Films? Eating out? Box sets? Drinking? She simply said that she was not into all that stuff and didn't have many interests. I couldn't believe how perfect she was.

When we reached the store, she looked at the items, considering them only based on their functionality and price. It didn't matter what a desk looked like, all that mattered was its price and durability. Style was not an issue. She inspected every item meticulously to see how well-built they were.

Ultimately, she opted for a small desk to do her university work on, a shelf for books, a collapsible chair and a fan heater - as she got cold even when it was summer.

It was a struggle to get all that stuff back on the bus, but she thanked me for my efforts by inviting me for a coffee in a nearby café after we had had dropped off the things at the house. She ordered a black coffee, so I ordered the same, even though I found the taste of coffee objectionable.

We mostly sat in silence at the coffee shop, which was fine by me, but at the same time, I still felt the need to pry and ask more questions. I brought up the subject of Guy. I said that I thought he was a fucking moron, and this made her giggle. I don't think that I had ever managed to make a woman giggle before that moment, so for me, it was a huge achievement. She said that she couldn't really comment as she didn't know him. I then asked her why she had turned down his invitation to go to the pub the other night, and she simply said that she didn't like pubs, so she didn't want to go. I told her that I didn't like pubs either, but she seemed unmoved by my admission. To her, it wasn't a big deal. Maybe she didn't come from a culture in which every single function or event either began or ended in a pub.

As we sat there drinking our black coffees, I suddenly felt the urge to tell her everything about myself, to just let loose. I wanted to tell her how I didn't fit in, how I didn't enjoy the things other people enjoyed, how in fact I didn't really enjoy anything at all, how I had never even kissed a woman, how I struggled every day to comprehend the nature of what people expected from others, and how I found social interaction simply exhausting.

But, I resisted. Instead, I sipped my black coffee and looked out of the window, imagining what would happen if the world just suddenly got sucked into a vortex and instantly vapourised. I looked back to my coffee and gazed into its unreflective black surface. If only I knew how to make Jana like me, if only I knew how to make her want me, if only I knew how to make her fuck me.

Soon, we had finished our coffees and decided to head home. As we left the coffee shop, I felt a strange sensation. Dare I say it, but I think that I had enjoyed my time with her. On some level, I enjoyed the day: the bus journey, the search for the cheapest and most durable furniture, the coffee. Yes, I had a good time. For fuck's sake, I liked it.

However, that was all about to change. When we got home the others had returned from their kick-about at the park. They were all in the kitchen, still messing around with the football and bragging about who was the best footballer.

They saw us walk in and called us both into the kitchen. Guy was smiling with his usual menacing glee. But, when he saw that Jana and I had just been out together, his eyes narrowed and his facial expression took a more sinister turn. I knew there would be no way that he would allow this union to remain unchallenged. We were two people who didn't fit into his mould and this threatened his world.

Everyone must be like Guy. Everyone must be like Guy. Everyone must be like Guy.

This was his mantra, and I'm sure he repeated this over and over in his head every second of the day.

"Hey, come and join us, you two," he said. "What have you two sneaky chimps been up to?"

I said that we had just been to buy some furniture for Jana's room.

"What? You should have come to me first! I know this super cool place where they sell vintage furniture. Everything there is like from the sixties or something and just experiencing that furniture is like taking a trip back in time. It would blow your mind!"

Jana replied saying that she had no interest in anything flash, and just wanted to find a functional set of furniture, which I had already helped her with perfectly. Fuck, I was falling in love.

"But, your room is like an experience," Guy protested. "That room is your whole life. How you feel in your room translates to how you feel in the outside world. You start with your home and make it how you want to feel. You want to return home to something that represents your personality, to a piece of yourself. Every single room is unique. It is a reflection of your individuality and shows the world who you are. How can you get that from a bland piece of furniture from a discount outlet store?"

I saw that Jana was beginning to be taken in by his spiel; her face showed signs of embarrassment with her choice of furniture, and she stuttered to provide an answer.

"Tell me what you like, Jana," Guy demanded. "We still need to do something to welcome you to the household. So tell me what you like. What gets Jana going?"

Jana became bashful and said that there was really nothing that she liked doing that they would enjoy.

"Ahh, so that must mean you like doing something. You just don't think that we would like it. Listen, Jana, we're all friends here and we are up for anything. We just love everything!" Guy said, to which the others all nodded in agreement.

I was just praying that Jana would not say anything back, to put Guy in his place. She was like me, she was not like him. Come on, Jana, tell him – tell that you don't like anything. But, she didn't. Instead, she coyly stated that she liked skating.

"Well, what's wrong with that?!" Guy said. "You know what, I just heard about this pop-up skating event going on near Shoreditch. It's like a seventies roller disco revival but on ice! It's only on for a few weeks and it's supposed to be super-ironic. We can all dress up! It will be off the hook! You're up for that, right? Jana?"

Jana smiled and nodded.

"Great! And I'm sure you'll want to come too, Nil?" Guy said, his tone dripping with sarcasm.

I looked at Jana. Could I really stomach this shit roller-disco-cum-ice-skating bollocks just to get close to her? I looked at Guy's smug face and told him that I would be coming. I would not let him win so easily.

We all went back to our rooms to get ready. I didn't need to change though, as I was intending to go dressed as I was. There was no point in changing my clothes as they all served the same function. I didn't have different clothes for different occasions. So, I just laid on my bed and waited for the others to do their thing. This downtime allowed me to pause and consider what I had just agreed to do. How was I going to make this work? I began to get jittery and nervous. I thought about pulling out and not going to the roller disco, but the idea of Guy having a whole night with Jana made me feel sick and compelled me to join them.

I heard Guy enter his room after having a shower and then heard him rummaging around. I guessed that he was carefully selecting his outfit and making sure everything was just right. But then, everything went silent for a minute and out of that silence, I heard something that I had never heard coming from his room before - it was the sound of porn. It sounded like he was watching a clip in which a man was brutally having sex with a woman - the man was inexplicably angry and she just seemed to be enjoying her role as a base sex object. I hated porn. I found it obscene and the antithesis of what was sexually arousing.

He was obviously watching it on his laptop, but the strangest aspect was that he had it on so loud. I had never heard him watching porn before, so why did he feel like he needed to increase the volume on this occasion? Did he have it on only for my benefit? What message was he trying to send to me?

The man in the clip continued to angrily pound the woman as she yelped and screamed for him to do it harder and harder. His disembodied grunting and groaning resonated through the walls and he kept shouting things like "bitch" and "little whore." Listening to the noises of that porn clip was particularly bizarre - it was like a perverse pantomime. A cartoonish charade that never exists in reality: brutal violence where no one is hurt or feels a single thing, just the perpetual pointless loop of fuck and get fucked. What someone could be getting from it, I did not know, but I suspected Guy was trying to send me a message. What message? At the time, I did not know, but I would find out later.

*

The ice skating event was just as horrific as I had imagined. The music was loud, the lighting was gaudy and everyone was wearing faux seventies costumes, except for Jana and I. Guy was in full seventies garb, but in a cool hipster way, not in the cheap fancy dress sense. The other housemates had cobbled together outfits from their wardrobes to create what they thought was the most seventies-looking attire. I wondered how Guy was so naturally prepared for this occasion - did he have a section of his wardrobe that was equipped with every fancy dress requirement?

We queued up, paid the admission fee and got our skates. I had never worn a pair of ice skates in my life. As we sat on the floor and put on the skates, I asked Jana if this was the type of place she usually went to in Estonia. She said that she just liked skating, regardless of the atmosphere. She added that she had never been to a place that mixed it with club music and fancy dress though. She wasn't sure that she liked it, but it was fine as long as she could do some skating. I was willing to accept that she liked the skating part and glad that she was indifferent to all the garish excess that this pop-up club had piled on top of it. There still might be hope for us yet, I thought.

I stood up and held onto the bar on the side of the rink to balance myself. I felt absurd in the skates and wanted nothing more than to put my normal shoes back on and escape from that place. But, I was determined to show Jana that I was capable of doing something that she liked.

She ignored my struggles with the skates and launched straight onto the rink, immediately gliding round and round effortlessly with all the other skaters. For the most part, the other skaters were joking, laughing and having a good time, but it seemed that they could only enjoy the skating through the filter of irony. They were lampooning seventies disco dancing moves and mockingly singing along to the songs that were playing.

The only person who was taking the whole thing seriously was Jana as she flew around the rink, weaving in and out of the piss-taking collective and getting annoyed if one of them obstructed her path.

Guy, Loz, Will, Oscar and I watched in silence as she completed several laps. It was rather bizarre to see someone take an activity so seriously when it was obviously designed to be parodied. But, she didn't seem to understand the irony involved and just continued in her own way, which I thought was endearing.

Eventually, Will, Loz and Oscar took to the rink and clumsily skated around while falling over and laughing. They were constantly trying to trip each other up and push each other over. Guy and I were still stationed on the side of the rink waiting to join the ring of circling skaters.

"You gonna join the party, Nil?" Guy asked me.

I simply said that I was happy just watching for a bit.

"That's your prerogative, bro," he said sharply and continued to stand watching the proceedings.

I briefly wondered if he had just realised that he had taken his own plan too far and didn't really have the stomach for this nonsense either. But, what he was really doing was waiting for Jana to complete her lap before beckoning her over.

She stopped and asked Guy what he wanted.

"Wow, Jana! You are amazing at this!" he gushed. "Look, I have to confess that I have never done this before, so I'm feeling a bit nervous. Could you show me the ropes? You know, just get me started?"

Jana agreed and slowly took Guy onto the rink. She instructed him on how to skate properly and supported his arm so he didn't fall over. Every now and again, Guy slipped and either fell or stopped himself from falling by grabbing on to her. They were both in hysterics every time this happened. Suspiciously, Guy's handle on the skates quickly became better and better, and he began skating around the rink with Jana on his arm as he ironically danced to the disco songs like the other skaters were doing. At first, she refused to participate in that stupid dancing, and just concentrated on skating. But, the more Guy persisted, the more her defences crumbled and she began to find his mock dancing hilarious. Soon, she was dancing to the music with him in her bashful way. She had a gleam on her face that indicated to me that she was enjoying the experience. They looked like they were a couple in a cheesy rom-com montage scene. Maybe that's where Guy had learned his moves. He had figured out the code: just give the situation a narrative. You could be anywhere doing anything, but if you create a narrative in the situation that people can follow, then they will be sucked in. I was incapable of doing such a thing though. I hated narratives and I hated stories; the only thing I understood about the world and time was that it was a pointless series of non-events that created a vacuous hole of meaninglessness.

I felt utterly defeated. Guy had seduced her with a good time and there was nothing at all that I could offer her to combat that. She didn't even look in my direction or notice if I was on the rink or anywhere on earth for that matter. I understood that she didn't care about me and there was no point fighting for it.

One last time, I looked at the people going round and round, laughing, joking and dancing. I saw Jana and Guy in the middle of the throng doing the same thing as all the rest - oh, how easily she was seduced. How could all these people find such enjoyment in the stupidest and simplest of things? For the first time, I wondered what it must feel like to be like them, to be able to enjoy life the way they do. Usually, I felt fine with this discord between me and everyone else, and in a way, it was my raison d'être - a way to set myself apart. But, after seeing Jana so easily absorbed and taken from my weak grasp, I felt an all-consuming depression filling my body. It was like my blood had spontaneously turned into molasses; a viscid substance that stuck to my organs and refused to flow around my veins. This stodginess in my body created a fog in my mind and I couldn't think of anything, couldn't feel anything, except the overwhelming need to go home and sleep.

I took off the skates, exchanged them for my own shoes and went home, leaving the others to have their fun.

On the journey home, I saw men and women together everywhere. On the Tube, I sat opposite a couple who looked like they had just started going out together. They were giggling and touching each other, staring longingly into each other's eyes. How did everyone else find it so easy to connect with one another, to find something in the other that they also saw in themselves? I could only ever see the other as some sort of alien to myself; they belonged somewhere different, in another reality to me. The plain fact was that without some interest in the culture into which you were born, then there is no way to connect to others within that culture. You are on the outside looking in, through an impenetrable shield. If you live outside it, then you cannot perform well at work, you cannot be important to anyone or anything, you cannot be interesting, you cannot find intimacy. To me, everything just seemed fake - a fraudulent reality or just an illusion. The ice skating, the Tube, the people and the relationships they create. It was all fake, a fabrication, a mould created out of perpetual chaos. Chaos ordered together to create a reality, to which we are all willing prisoners.

When I returned to my room, I looked at the insects on the shelves and knew that in the insect kingdom, I would have died long ago. An insect that doesn't conform dies and bears no offspring. It is as simple as that. Maybe I was already in an acrylic box just like they were.

I fell into bed without bothering to undress and went straight to sleep. It was a deep, dark and dreamless sleep. Later, I was rudely awoken from this blissful slumber to the sound of the housemates coming home. They were all drunk and in high spirits. Jana was with them and sounded drunk too; it seemed like she had really come out of her shell during the evening. They went into the kitchen to continue the drinking and after a while, they all retreated to their rooms.

Thankful that they had all finally gone to bed, I closed my eyes and tried to get back to sleep. But, when I was on the verge of sleep, I heard the sound of porn coming from Guy's room again. I couldn't believe that he would put it on so loud at that time of night. This porn wasn't as violent and grotesque as the other porn though. This time, it was more realistic - just the grunts and groans of two people having sex. I tried to block it out, but I couldn't, the noise was just too intrusive and I was getting sick of Guy's bullshit. I decided that it was enough, so I got out of bed with the intention of telling him to turn the volume down. I was going to tell him that watching porn that loud was disrespectful and he needed to turn it off right away. I marched out of my room and turned to his door, my fist poised in a knocking position. But, there was no need to knock, his door was already wide open. I looked inside and saw that it wasn't porn that Guy was watching - he was fucking for real, and it was with Jana. He had her bent over on the bed while he pounded her from behind. Jana's face was buried deep into the mattress and Guy was mesmerised by the sight of his dick penetrating her vagina. He had her arse cheeks pulled apart as far as he could, so the sight of his dick entering her was not obstructed in the slightest. He wanted to experience fucking her to its fullest and store it in his mind for future use, I thought. I couldn't believe what I was seeing and couldn't understand why he had left the door open. Did he simply forget or just not care? Was it really a performance? Did he want me to watch? Maybe he wanted to demonstrate his victory over me and show me all the things that I could have if I followed his way of life? Whatever the reason, it was fucking creepy.

He turned his head towards me and glared into my eyes. He was not surprised to see me there. In fact, it was like he knew I had been there watching him all along. At first, his face was blank and expressionless, before it contorted into one of his huge shit-eating grins. His glowing teeth shone through the dimmed light and mocked my very being. I frowned and shook my head, to which he pouted and blew a kiss in my direction. He then juddered and his whole body spasmed and I wondered what was going on until he removed his dick from Jana and came all over her back and arse. Jana's face was still buried in the mattress while Guy arched his head back and expelled a loud, relieved groan.

I retreated back to my room and laid on the bed. I thought that would be the end of it, but five minutes later, the noises started up again and they went through a whole new session. Then, half an hour after that, another session began. The noises were unbearable - traumatic even. The vision of Guy ejaculating over Jana replayed in a repeated loop in my head as their disembodied grunts and groans saturated the air. I could even smell it; their fluids interchanging within one another - semen, sweat and discharge. The noises grew louder and louder and taunted me with all the things I had never had, and never would have. All I wanted at that moment was to be in Guy's place and I never believed that I would think like that.

Finally, their fuck-filled night came to an end, but there was no way I was going to be able to get back to sleep so easily. Thoughts of Jana and Guy swirled in my head. I wondered if Guy even liked Jana, or if he was fucking her just because he could. I wondered if Jana had felt any attraction to me at any point, or if I was simply deluded from the start? I had no answers to any of these questions. That was all I had - questions. Question after question, yet no answers.

The insects were all looking at me again. Their black beady eyes constantly returning my gaze. What did they want from me? Were they researching me? Judging me? Or just watching on in morbid curiosity?

What started as a good day ended as a nightmare all thanks to Guy and his dislike of me. I was seemingly powerless against him. He had won every battle, and I was devoid of ideas on how to challenge him. He was strong and I was weak.

Thud-thud. Thud-thud. The low level thudding from Guy's room began again. What was that noise?! Could Guy be so crazy as to stay awake after having sex with Jana and start that thudding again just to wear me down even more? That thudding rattled me to the core. It continued for what felt like hours and seemed to grow

louder and louder. THUD-THUD. THUD-THUD. THUD-THUD. EN-JOY. EN-JOY. EN-JOY.
FUCK YOU GUY!

*

The sleepless night was capped off by a text from my boss. He needed me to cover someone else's shift. I jumped at the chance, even though I was exhausted. I was running desperately low on funds and needed the money. But, more importantly, I needed to get out of the house and avoid seeing Guy and particularly Jana. I just needed to avoid her at all costs now. It would be hard, but I just couldn't bear to see her face or, worse yet, see her being intimate with Guy.

I put my work clothes on and made the strongest coffee I could, even though I hated the stuff, in order to try and shake myself out of my dazed state. But, it was no use. For the entire journey to work, my eyes were half shut and all I could think about was Guy and Jana, in bed, together. They were probably fucking each other right now, I thought. I tried to put myself in Guy's place and imagined that I was fucking her instead of him. What must it have felt like? I couldn't even imagine. I longed to know how it felt to wake up next to Jana, but again, I couldn't begin to imagine it. Guy was the one who had that privilege, not me. What if I could be like Guy and seduce people the way he did?

I stopped myself. These were dangerous thoughts. When I started to imagine what it would be like to be Guy, then something was definitely wrong. I cleared my head and tried not to think about Guy and his dick ejaculating over Jana's arse, and prepared myself for a day at work. I was determined to work well on the shifts I was given in the hope that I could impress my boss and increase my chances of getting more regular shifts. I knew the surly fucker didn't like me though. He was a football-loving meathead, and if you couldn't have a conversation about the football, then you were a suspicious character in his eyes. For a man who was merely a passive supporter at the games, he sure thought highly of himself when his team won, or angry at himself when they lost. When I first starting working there, I absent-mindedly mentioned that I thought football, or sport in general, was the epitome of tedium and asininity. I don't think he quite understood what I meant, but he got the gist that I didn't like it, and from that moment on, he had always had it in for me. He was always looking for a way to criticise or penalise me in some way. However, on that day, I was going to make sure that he saw how well I was working and realise that I was indispensable. It was an admirable plan, but it didn't materialise as I intended. Instead, I achieved the opposite of what I set out to do and spent the day fucking everything up.

The tiredness had really consumed me, and regardless how hard I tried, I could not get Guy and Jana out of my mind. It also didn't help that they had changed the working system that week, so I couldn't run on autopilot as usual. The boss quickly showed me how to use the new system, but the information did not stick in my preoccupied mind. When I got stuck, I asked my co-workers to remind me how the new system worked, but their help was limited at best. For the first time, I regretted not making any friends in that place. I made mistake after mistake and this did not go unnoticed by my boss, who was on my back for the entire day. He also quickly cottoned on to my fatigued condition and told me that I shouldn't have agreed to come into work if I was I not in a fit state to do so. By the end of the day, he was fuming at me and sent me home an hour early, telling me not to expect any future shifts, and that was that - no more job.

I trudged home with my back arched forward and head hung low. I was the walking cliché of dejection. But I couldn't help it, things were looking bleak. I only had a small amount of savings remaining and couldn't envision how I was going to pay the rent after next month, let alone eat. And, I could find no solace at that house, it had become a constant source of pain and frustration. Frankly, I could not handle living there anymore.

I walked all the way back home, which was about a four-mile journey. I was utterly spent by the time I approached the house, but when I saw it and thought about all the things that it contained, I just couldn't bear to go inside. Then, in my enervated state, I made a rash decision. I decided I would never return to that house. I concluded that I was soon to be homeless anyway, so there was no point in delaying the inevitable and it was better to just get on with it. I was done with that place and everyone in it. I didn't even bother going in to get any of my stuff as I didn't want to run the risk of bumping into any of my housemates. There would be no use for a collection of dead insects or a mini fridge on the streets, anyhow.

I searched the parks, backroads, alleyways and shop fronts for a suitable place to set up camp. There was nothing that took my fancy until I stumbled upon a side road that was occupied by small rented garages. I rattled the up-and-over doors on each garage to see if any were open, and to my surprise, I found a dilapidated one that was loose. I could pull up the door a sufficient amount to crawl underneath and get inside. It was perfect in there - exactly what I was looking for. It was bare yet sheltered and looked like it hadn't been used in a long time. I decided that this was to be my new home. I had my bank card and five pounds in cash in my wallet. I decided to save my bank card as long as possible, but I would spend the five pounds immediately on food and vital supplies.

I went to the local convenience shop and bought the cheapest, longest-lasting food available which also didn't require cooking. That basically meant cheap tinned meats and beans. The five pounds didn't buy much, but I knew that I would have to become accustomed to rationing and eating sparsely on the streets anyway.

On the way back, I stopped off at a charity clothing bin on the street and rummaged through the overspill in front of it, picking myself out some warm clothes. There was even a blanket among all the clothing, which I snapped up instantly. I returned to the garage with my swag and settled in for my first night. I ate a meal that consisted of corned beef and cold sweet corn. It was vile, and I briefly thought of what the housemates might be cooking up in the kitchen that evening, but I forced that out of my mind. I did not want to think about them or their lifestyle anymore, I needed to just get on with my new life now. This was it, right here and now, everything that I had dreamed of: solitude and removal from the suffocating pressure and demands of society. Sure, it was a cold, dank and uncomfortable hovel, but this place had no parties, no flamboyant dinners, no talking, no socialising, no pretence, no bullshit whatsoever.

I laid down and began to spot all the various insects that were cohabiting with me. There were *Musca domestica*, a single *Vespula vulgaris*, many *Lasius niger*, and even a *Forficula auricularia* scuttling up the wall. In any other setting, these insects would be considered pests or vermin and would be exterminated. But there in that garage, we were all welcome. The insects and I, living side by side as perfect housemates. They didn't expect anything of me and the feeling was mutual. It was the perfect match.

I closed my eyes and smiled. I was finally home.

*

It was a hard night's sleep. The concrete floor was unforgiving on my body, which was used to soft mattresses. It also became cold in the early hours of the morning, which I didn't expect at that time of year. I couldn't imagine what it would be like in the winter months. I felt even more jaded than the previous day, but I reassured myself with the fact that it was only my first night sleeping rough and I would, in time, get used to the new circumstances. I needed to find more blankets and soft bedding to facilitate a better night's sleep. I could spend my whole day hunting for useful items if I wanted, as I had nothing better to do now. I had nowhere to be and nowhere to go. It was a sense of freedom that I initially revelled in.

My breakfast consisted of the second portion of the corned beef and sweet corn from the previous night. It tasted even worse in the morning as my mouth felt like shit in a microwave. I had not even considered what I would do about brushing my teeth when I made my initial decision to leave the house, but it was now a pressing issue. What would I do about it? Even if I bought a toothbrush and toothpaste, I couldn't afford to sustain buying them in the long run, so it would be something that I would eventually have to forgo. Fuck it, I thought, let my teeth rot and my breath stink of arsehole. Good riddance to dental hygiene - that was for those who conformed to society anyhow.

As I ate my disgusting breakfast, I continued to watch the inhabiting creatures.

After breakfast, I lifted the door to the garage and peered out to see if anyone was around. It was all clear, so I crawled out from under the door and stood in the morning mist. I wasn't sure of the time, but it felt early - very early. I stretched out my bruised muscles and bones, preparing myself for the day ahead. I looked around and realised that I had absolutely nowhere to go, nothing that needed urgently doing, and it was still way too early, so I crawled back into the garage and decided to wait inside for a while longer. So, I sat there and waited, and waited, and waited...

The battery on my phone had died overnight, so I had no idea what time it was or how long I had been sitting there, but it felt like a long time.

After a while, I guessed at around eight or eight-thirty, I picked myself up and went out for a walk. I surmised that it must've been around that time, as there was an immense struggle going on amongst the commuters trying to get to work. People were striding along the streets in a single-minded focus and were crawling over each other to get into the Tube stations, on buses and into taxis, and were queuing up like dumb fucks for a hit of overpriced coffee. Fucking locusts, I thought. Vile and disgusting creatures, the lot of them. I hated their suits and stupid clothes, their perfumed stench, and fucking moronic sandals that exposed their gnarled-up feet. They really believed they were doing something important. I began to revel in my role as a homeless indigent outsider. I spat on the floor as I walked. I looked them straight in the eyes as I passed and thought to myself that the only thing that we all have common is that we're all dying together. Other than that, I couldn't even begin to comprehend what was behind their empty eyes: two slots that were a gateway to a gaping void of nothingness. And, even with all the shit that they told themselves to provide assurance for their existence, they couldn't escape the truth that they all truly knew, but would never admit: we are the emptiness itself, the black hole at the core of nature. What set me apart is that I knew this and now accepted it, embraced it even. I was on the fringes. No job, no home, no family, no friends, no access to the internet, no nothing. Just a walking skin bag of flesh and shit. So, fuck it, and fuck them all.

My anger subsided when the commotion of rush hour had subsided and the streets had emptied out, which meant I could roam freely again. I searched around for some more charity bins and extracted what I could out of them, but it was slim pickings as the overspills had been cleaned up, either by the charity workers or because others like me had already looted what they could. Even so, I still managed to find a mud-splattered jacket as well as a piss-stained blanket. They were good finds, but I needed something to use for bedding more than anything. I wandered down a back street and found a skip behind a convenience shop that was filled with cardboard boxes. I took them out, flattened them and then carried as many as I could back to the garage.

I used five of the cardboard boxes to build a mattress, leaving one to use as a cover, which I would use in conjunction with the piss-stained wool blanket I had found at the charity bin. After it was all set up, I admired my handiwork and decided to take a nap to give it a test run. The sleep was much better than I had managed the previous night, but I could still feel the cold unforgiving concrete making its presence known underneath.

When I woke up in what I guessed was late afternoon, I heard some rattling in one of the nearby garages. A man was talking on his phone and revving up his car for some inexplicable reason. I remained quiet and just waited for him to do his thing and leave, which he did soon after. I was annoyed that he had interrupted my sleep, but I knew that I would just have to put up with that kind of thing. Now that I was awake, I couldn't get back to sleep and felt groggy and uncomfortable. There was no way of ever getting comfortable in that garage, and I knew that I would just have to put up with that too. I watched the insects for a while and saw how easily they adapted to their environment and how comfortable they were with the surroundings. They didn't need soft mattresses, cotton blankets, warm clothes or hot food. They just got on with it, just like I would have to now. I would have to put my admiration of the insects into practice and act as they did. I would have to adapt - there was no other choice.

I watched them with fascination for a while until out of nowhere, I desperately needed to take a shit. That was another thing I hadn't considered. Where was my toilet going to be? There was nowhere to go in the garage except straight on the floor. I would have to do it somewhere outside. I remembered that there was an overgrown alleyway nearby. I would have to go somewhere in the alley and wipe my arse with a leaf or grass or something like that.

But, just as I was about to crawl out under the garage door, I heard some voices approaching. It sounded like a group of boys, teenagers, I thought. They were loud and obnoxious, spouting phrases and using terminology that I could not understand. All I knew was that it sounded threatening. I concluded that it would be a bad idea to be seen, so I retreated into the garage and attempted to hold back on the shit that had already pushed itself halfway down my colon. It sounded like there were three of them in total and they were crudely conversing about their chances of getting some "pussy" that night. It was all macho posturing. They then proceeded to light up a joint. The billowing smoke found its way into the garage and filled the air, which meant that I had to hold back all my urges to cough in order to retain my cover. The joint didn't seem to mellow them at all - they just continued with their loud brash conversation, showing each other photos of past "pussy" and potential candidates who would be future "pussy". They then turned to texting and calling the current "pussy" for meet ups. Finally, they managed to convince some girls to meet them. I hoped that they would leave to meet them somewhere else, but instead, they talked the girls into to coming to the garages. One of them then left to get some beer, so I realised that they were going to be there for a while. I held on to the shit as best as I could and laid back down on the cardboard bed, staring at the garage ceiling. Even though I was homeless, I still had to put up with neighbours, I thought. Was there no way to escape from them all?

I laid there, my stomach growling, listening to them talk nonsense. I listened to every sip of beer and exaggerated burp, every forced roar of laughter, and every word of self-assertive bullshit they spewed. When the girls turned up, I listened to their over-performative conversation techniques that were intended to impress them. I listened as they all smoked more joints and drank more beer, forced more laughter and talked even more bullshit. And, finally, I listened as one of the boys pissed all over the door to my garage and smashed a beer bottle on the floor right outside. Thankfully, they left after that.

My stomach was bursting, so I pulled open the garage door and crawled outside through the piss and shattered beer bottle. I ran to the alleyway where I finally managed to relieve myself of the shit while also managing to sting my buttocks on some nettles in the process. I also had a pain in my knee, so I checked it out and saw that it was bleeding from crawling through the glass. I went into the street and inspected it under a street light. A piece of glass was embedded into the skin. I slowly yet painfully removed the glass and compressed the wound as it gushed with blood. I limped back to the garage and collapsed on the cardboard bed. A rancid odour of shit, piss, blood, beer, smoke and corned beef filled the air. I felt light-headed and wrapped my knee with a charity bin T-shirt to stem the flow of blood pouring out. I was aching, cold and uncomfortable. I had never cared previously about the weather, but after spending the night in the garage, the cold had begun to bother me. It crawled up and under my skin and filled every sinew, bone and blood cell. Even though it was nearing summer and some of the days were temperate, that night it turned wet with a chilling wind. Everything was moist, which added to the feeling of cold and discomfort.

There was nothing left to do except try and get some sleep, so I did the best I could and wrapped myself in every item of clothing I had and settled on the cardboard bed. The wind and rain rattled the garage. I closed my eyes and readied myself for another torrid night of sleep.

*

The next day, I woke early again, wet, freezing and sodden with blood. I blubbered for a second and then forced myself to pull it together. I inspected my knee and saw that the wound had at least stopped bleeding, even though it was raw and needed disinfecting.

I consumed a breakfast of tinned mackerel in tomato sauce while indulging in my only entertainment - watching the insects. They had been feasting on my blood during the night, sucking down its warm sugary goodness, getting bloated on the fat of the land. I noticed that a family of *Blattella germanica* had joined our nest, probably enticed by the lake of red nourishment flowing from my knee. One of them stopped and looked at me. It seemed as though it was sizing me up, planning its meal. Maybe in the night, all the insects in that garage would swarm over me and gnaw through my flesh like a juicy human steak, I thought. Now that they had the taste of blood, they craved more.

I shivered at the roach's icy stare, with its black eyes already devouring me. I retaliated by shooing it away, although I knew that little fucker was now off to give the other insects ideas about gobbling me up.

As I watched the roach scuttle off, I noticed something in the garage that I hadn't noticed before - a plug socket. Electricity would be a handy thing to have as I could use it to greatly enhance my living space. I knew that if I could sneak back into the house, I could grab some useful things, retrieve some essentials. I could get my travel hob, steal that portable heater from Jana's room and take my bedside lamp. Not much - just a few things to facilitate the transition into my new life. I hadn't anticipated just how difficult sleeping rough would be. It was all too much too soon. So, I made up my mind to go back and take the things that I needed from the house.

It was still early morning by the time I reached the house. I knew that all the housemates would still be inside, so I went to the alleyway at the back of the house to wait there.

The alleyway still contained the remnants of Pablo's leaving party. It was littered with beer cans, chicken bones, cigarette butts, and crisp packets. There was even a used condom festering in the undergrowth. I crouched down and shuffled up to a gap in the fence so I could peer through. No-one was in the kitchen yet, so I presumed that they were still all in bed. My knee was sore and crouching only served to rip the wound open even more. I wouldn't be able to remain in that position for a length of time, so I swept all the litter to one side and knelt on a patch of grass with all my weight shifted onto my good knee. I continued to look through the gap and waited for any activity.

One by one, the housemates started getting up. I knew this because I watched as they shuffled dozily into the kitchen and made themselves breakfast. The first to emerge was Loz, followed by Oscar, and then Will. I assumed that they would follow their usual routines and leave the house not long after finishing their breakfasts. There was no sign of Guy or Jana yet. Jana's bedroom window backed onto the garden, but her curtains were drawn. Guy's room looked out to the front so I couldn't see if there was any activity in his room either. I wondered if they were together in one of the rooms. It was likely that they were an item by now. A pang of jealousy shot through my body at the thought of Jana hanging lovingly off of Guy's arm. But, I couldn't let it bother me. I had a new life now that could never include someone like Jana, so I just needed to get over it.

Finally, Guy appeared in the kitchen. He was on his own and already dressed to leave the house. I watched as he made himself a herbal tea and some sort of avocado and poached egg on sourdough bread concoction. Even though he was on his own, he still acted like he was being watched by a television crew. Every movement he made seemed rehearsed and careful, and the breakfast he made for himself was needlessly intricate for something that was just going to be scoffed down his gullet moments later. He positioned everything on the kitchen table perfectly and held up his phone to take a photo of his "masterpiece". He studied the photo and decided it wasn't good enough, so he rearranged the breakfast items and took another photo. What a fucking cock, I thought. After the photo session was over, he relaxed and then proceed to eat the breakfast like an automaton. He seemed to take no pleasure in the taste and exhibited no reaction to the flavours. It was the first time I had ever seen him not express joy or excitement about what he was doing. For the first time, he almost seemed normal. After his breakfast, he cleaned up his plates and left the house, so that meant that only Jana was left.

I waited and waited, then finally I perked up as I saw Jana's silhouette at the bottom of the stairs. But, instead of coming into the kitchen, all I saw of her was the back of her head, probably going straight out of the front door without bothering with breakfast.

I got up off the floor and walked out of the alleyway and around the street to the front of the house. I opened the door and went up to my room as quickly as I could. I rummaged around, searching for the best things that I could take with me back to the garage. I grabbed my plastic tub and filled it with my travel hob, my bedside lamp, my phone charger, a bottle of water, some tins of food, a small pot, some essential kitchen utensils and a few items of clothing. I also took one of the pillows from my bed and tried to get into Jana's room to take her heater, but her door was locked.

A pain emanated from my knee. I looked down at it and saw that it had started to bleed again. I was also well aware that I utterly stank. I was caked in all kinds of bodily fluids - I desperately needed a shower and to clean and dress the wound.

I came out of my room and went to the bathroom, but just as I began to undress, I heard a key rattling in the front door lock. I stopped what I was doing and listened as the person entered the kitchen. I put the clothes that I had just taken off back on and carefully crept back to my room. I pushed the door shut as delicately as I could and wondered how I was going to get out of there. I thought that I would just wait until whoever it was went into their room and then I could sneak out the front door. But, within minutes, I heard another person come through the front door, followed by mumblings in the kitchen; it sounded like it was Guy and one of the other housemates. Soon, they were making their way upstairs and into Guy's room. Their voices were clear, so I assumed that Guy had left the door to his room open. I couldn't let them know of my presence and wanted to get out of the house as soon as possible.

I looked at my window and thought of my previous failed attempt to jump out of it. It now seemed like a good idea again. But, what if this time I had something to assist my descent? Suddenly, my other idea about abseiling down the side of the building popped into my mind. I still had the hoses that I had used for my plumbing system rolled up in the cupboard, so I pulled one of them out, tied it to the base of my bed and jammed the bed tight up against the wall. I then opened the window and slung the hose out, allowing it to drape down to the garden floor. I realised that I wouldn't be able to abseil down the side of the building while carrying my things, so I reeled back the hose. I tied the hose around the plastic tub that contained all the possessions that I wanted to take with me and then lowered it out of the window and onto to the garden floor.

I looked out of the window and experienced flashbacks of my swollen ankle. I tugged on the hose and it seemed sturdy enough. It should be able to hold me for one trip, I thought. I carefully climbed out with one hand on the hose and the other holding onto the sill. I once again gauged the strength of the hose before letting go of the sill and allowing the hose to hold my weight. The hose was not up to the job and stretched immediately. I slipped down the wall as the hose elongated, and just as I was about half a metre from the ground, the hose snapped from the knot at the base of the bed and I fell the rest of the way, although I landed planted on my feet this time. I stood shaking, incredulous that I had just descended that wall with a hose and escaped unharmed from the experience.

I took the hose and threw it over the fence into the alleyway. Then, I picked up the plastic tub and made my way back to the garage, beaming proudly as a result of the feat I had just pulled off. Ok, so I didn't manage to clean myself up or steal the heater, but overall, I did well. When I got back to the garage, I unpacked my spoils and plugged in the lamp, preparing for some light. It didn't work. I thought that it might have broken, so I tried the phone charger and then the hob. Nothing. The socket didn't work: there was no power. Why had I not considered that would be the case?

The family of German cockroaches were scuttling around inanely. The same one from before stopped and looked at me again. I laid back down on the cardboard bed and now hoped that he was indeed planning to eat me. Just do it, I thought. Devour me. Destroy me. Enjoy my flesh. Just get it over and done with.

*

I woke up later in the afternoon. There was a rattling outside the door again. I sat up and rubbed my fists into my eyes. My head was foggy and my knee throbbed with pain. Was it those kids outside again, here to drink beer, smoke drugs and brag about getting "pussy"? Maybe, it was another homeless man trying to shack up as my roommate? Or maybe, just an opportunistic thief?

It turned out to be none of those, but each of those options would have been preferable to what was actually awaiting. The door flung open to reveal two huge meatheads who stood there towering over me. Their faces contorted into a grimace as soon as they saw me sitting on the floor. One of them pinched his nose to block out the smell that I had generated inside over the previous few days. The other screamed at me for having the temerity to sleep in the garage that he had paid for with his own hard-earned money. He called me all kinds of insulting names and berated me for not having a job and being "scum". He peppered almost every sentence with the word "scum" and managed to amplify his anger towards me by just using his own words.

I cowered in the corner, not saying a thing - I just waited for his tirade to cease. I knew that any words I would say would only make the situation worse, so I waited for him to vent his rage. Once he had calmed down, I began to edge for the door. The man who was holding his nose suggested to his friend that they had to teach me a lesson, otherwise I would just come back the next day or the day after that. They wanted to make sure they got rid of me for good. They both agreed that there was the only one course of action that could be employed in dealing with utter scum like me. I didn't know exactly what form this course of action would take, but I knew it was going to be something bad and I didn't want to stay and find out. So, I jumped off the floor and darted for the door, which took them both by surprise. I evaded them both and escaped out of the garage, but my knee was so crippled with pain that I couldn't run very fast and one of them quickly caught me and wrestled to the floor. He complained to his friend about how much I stank and that I was worse than an animal. He kept me pinned to the floor by digging his knee deep into my back, causing a sharp pain that radiated throughout my body. I was then made to watch as the other one rummaged through the things that I had earlier retrieved from the house. He mocked every item for being rubbish and stamped on everything, making sure it was all thoroughly destroyed. However, he seemed quite taken with the portable cooking hob and claimed that it could be of some use to him, so he put it to one side.

By this time, my whole body was numb from the knee in my spine and I began to scream, demanding to be let free. The man slapped me on the back of the head and told me to shut up. I began to blubber and pleaded for him to let me go, but instead of appealing to any sympathy he may have had, it just made him laugh and slap me about even more.

I was finally let off the floor and helped to stand up, but this was only so one of them could sling me back into the garage and against the back wall. My body thudded against the brick, my arm taking most of the impact. I yelped and collapsed on the floor. The next thing I felt was a boot to the face. This time it was my lip that took the impact, splitting it and causing blood to pool in my mouth. I choked and spat the blood on the floor. I heard their laughter in my ringing ears. I didn't realise torture could be so funny and pleasurable to others. They seemed to be genuinely enjoying the sight of my blood and pain. I looked around for the insects, but they had all gone. They did not stay around to spectate, their plans of devouring me in my sleep were over; the humans were going to devour me instead.

One of the men then decided it would be funny to take my shoes off my feet and spank me over the arse with them. They cracked obscene jokes as they did this, pretending that I was the sexual object in some sort of dominatrix porn. They then made me smell the inside of the shoes by pressing them forcefully into my bloodied face. The more they humiliated me, the more they laughed and enjoyed themselves.

I felt as though I had ceased to be human, that any shred of humanity I still possessed had been ripped away. I had no connection to my mind or body - I just was. Just a creature that had no understanding of what I was experiencing, or the reason why I was experiencing it. There was just darkness in front of my eyes even though I could see what was around me. I was deaf even though I could hear their laughter. My body felt numb even though it was bursting with pain. It all shrunk into nothing and left only one thing behind: raw instinct.

This raw instinct guided my teeth onto one of the men's legs and made me bite hard. I bit so fucking hard that my teeth sunk into his flesh and struck bone. The man roared in agony and anger, and before they had a chance to hold me back, I found the strength to run. The instinct allowed me to run without pain and so fast that they were unable to catch me. They gave up on the chase after a short while. I could hear their screams fading into the distance and when the screams had died out completely, my body suddenly realised that it was mortal and I collapsed in anguish.

I laid prone on the hard concrete floor. The transition from extreme stress to relief caused my bowels and bladder to release themselves - piss trickled down my leg and shit filled my underwear. My bare feet were red and raw. My arm bruised and swollen. My knee a mess of pus and exposed flesh. My muscles knotted and stretched. My body in atrophy. My mind a traumatised wreck. The humiliation was total and complete.

I didn't know where to go or what to do. The only thing I could think of was to go back to the house, back to my room. It was that or die there on the pavement. So, I picked myself up and hobbled through the streets, my mangled body struggling with every step. I was completely ignored by everyone I passed. I was invisible to them, existing outside of their society, outside of their humanity. No-one stopped me to see if I needed help - I was avoided at all costs. I was a threat to the enjoyment of their evening. They didn't want their coffee and cake time, their pub meet, their movie night, their restaurant reservations, their pleasant evening walk punctured by me or anything close to my reality. To help me would be to acknowledge my existence, and what a painful truth that would be.

I finally made it to the house, but I couldn't bear to make an entrance like that. I couldn't let them see me that way. I had been humiliated enough that day, I couldn't take even more. Instead, I went down the alleyway behind the house and knelt at the fence, peering through the gap like I had done earlier. This time, I saw that Jana's curtains were open and that the light was on in her room. I watched her as she went about her life, oblivious of my gaze upon her. It was so good to see her. I felt better just watching. Soon she began to undress and even though I knew it was morally wrong to continue watching, I couldn't turn my gaze. She took off all her clothes until she was completely naked. I wanted her more than anything I had ever known. At that moment, something changed in me. I realised that I did not want to be that person anymore. I was tired of being me, being out of society, always on the fringes. I wanted to know what it was like to be with Jana, I wanted to know what it was like to be a human like other people. I wanted to know what it was like to enjoy things and experience life like the others. It was either change or stay as I was. To be out of society was too painful, too much to bear, too traumatic. I was living a life of pain and discomfort; if I conformed, then I could have it all. The only thing I would have to sacrifice was my freedom. As my entire being throbbed in pain, I concluded that freedom could go fuck itself. I pulled out my suddenly erect penis and masturbated to the sight of Jana walking around naked in her room. The thrill of masturbating to this vision dulled the ache of my body. After Jana had changed into her nightwear, I ejaculated and then fell to the ground and passed out - asleep or unconscious, or both. All I knew was that it was the most restful sleep I had ever had.

THE INDIVIDUAL

When I awoke from that sleep, everything had changed.
I opened my eyes and found myself face down in moss, leaves, grass and mud. My lips were kissing the dirt like a man begging for redemption. I pulled myself off the floor and spat out the all the earthy shit that had accumulated in my mouth over the course of the night. I rubbed my eyes to clear out the grit, but only succeeded in rubbing more into them. I looked at my body and saw that I was caked in all kinds of bodily fluids and muck. I also reeked of every bad smelling awful thing possible. The wound on my knee was still raw and was seeping septic yellow pus. My busted lip was pulsating and swollen. My arm was a useless appendage, it just hung beside my body with no sensation or feeling - just a dead log of flesh. Basically, I

was a fucking mess. A pathetic wretch of a human being. A man of no substance or reason to exist. My current principles and philosophy on life had directly led me to this situation and I decided that I had had enough. No more would I be cast out into the fringes. No more would I align myself with the insect world. No more would I let myself suffer the hardships of being an outcast.

It was time to change and begin anew.

I walked out of the alleyway and around to the front of the house. I opened the front door and entered. I didn't know what time it was, but I didn't care if there was anyone home or not; nonetheless, the house seemed unoccupied. I went straight up to my room, tore all my clothes off and discarded them in a heap in the corner. In my naked state, I went through the landing and into the bathroom.

Firstly, I sat on the toilet and released my bowels. The piss and shit flowed from my body, relieving the tension in my stomach. After I was finished, I didn't bother wiping my arse; instead, I simply got into the shower, turned on the tap and allowed the jets of water to soothingly wash my entire body. There was a full bottle of shower gel on the side which was not mine, but I ended up using the whole bottle, cleaning every single orifice and gap and crevice on my body. I reached down to my knee and squeezed all the pus out of it, cleaning it vigorously. I found a small piece of broken glass embedded in the wound and pulled it loose, which caused the gash to pour with blood again. The bloodletting was actually soothing and it allowed me to clean deep inside and remove all the dirt. I turned the shower to the coldest it would go and let the icy streams cool the burning sensation on my lip. The cold water was also refreshing on my reddened eyeballs. I massaged my dead arm with someone's coarse loofah and gradually brought it back to life. I also cried uncontrollably as I did all of this; I don't know why, but that too was therapeutic.

After the shower, I climbed out and dried myself off. I searched through the bathroom cupboard and found a first aid kit. I smeared antiseptic cream all over the knee wound and then dressed it with cotton and a bandage. Once the wound was taken care of, I squeezed a quarter of a tube of toothpaste in my mouth and violently brushed until blood appeared on the gums. I then flossed the gaps between every tooth and gargled a cup's worth of mouthwash. When that was done, I brushed my teeth once more just to be sure. Finally, I shaved off all the stubble that I had grown over the last week and moisturised my skin until it was gleaming and revitalised.

After I was finished in the bathroom, I wrapped the towel around my waist, went to the kitchen and retrieved a bag of frozen peas from the freezer and a bin bag from the cupboard. I brought the items back upstairs to my room, stuffed the soiled and rancid clothes into the bin bag and then set the frozen peas against my swollen lip.

I changed the sheets on my bed with fresh ones and then laid down upon them feeling fresh and new, like being born into a new world. The calm generated by being back in comfortable surroundings allowed me to drift into sleep. But, this was not an empty sleep like the previous night or indeed a dreamless sleep for that matter; this sleep was full of manic dreams and visions of things that I couldn't comprehend.

When I awoke, it was afternoon and the house was still empty. I pulled on some clean clothes and went into the kitchen. I made myself a coffee and drank it while sitting at the dining table, which I had never done before. For the first time, I had no fear of someone coming home and having to engage in a conversation with them. As I sat there, I realised that I liked the feeling of being in a different room to my bedroom and drinking that coffee. It made a change from being all cramped up on my bed. I even found the coffee more palatable than usual.

After I had finished the coffee, I washed the cup and searched around the kitchen, looking in the cupboards and fridge to see what foods the others had bought. It was not the kind of cheap, long-lasting, tinned goods that I would buy. Their foods looked fresh and had classy packaging. The packaging itself looked good enough to eat.

As I was looking through the cupboards, I came across a stack of Guy's cookbooks. I pulled them out and leafed through the pages to see the kinds of things that he had been making. The recipes that he had tried had been tagged with post-it notes in which he had written reminders and suggestions. They said things like "needs more cumin," or "remember to reduce for longer than the recipe says". Each note also had various little handwritten emojis. I came across a recipe that had a post-it note with the words "must try this recipe someday!!!!" written in thick ink - it was a Cajun Gumbo. I briefly glanced over the method and then took a photo of the ingredients needed to make it. Maybe it was time I got involved with the cooking, I thought.

I grabbed my wallet and went to the upscale supermarket that Guy frequented. It would be my first time ever at that particular chain, as I usually went to the low-price stores looking for value over quality. I picked up a basket and wandered through the aisles, trying to source the ingredients needed to make the gumbo recipe. It was an arduous task, as I didn't even know what some of the ingredients were, let alone what they looked like. I had never heard of cayenne pepper before, and what the fuck were bay leaves? This was way beyond my level of cooking expertise.

I found a store employee who was stacking shelves and I asked him where I could find some of the ingredients that were in the recipe. He escorted me to each ingredient, ushering me through the aisles that were filled with a dizzying array of product choices. I just soaked it all in, it was hypnotic; all the colours, promotions, tempting aromas of coffee, freshly baked breads and grilled meats. It was all perfectly presented to entice the senses. I thought back to my meal of Spam and cold corn that I had eaten in the isolation of the garage and how I never wanted to resort to living such a life again. I wanted all these new and enticing things and desired to shop in places like this supermarket. It felt good to be in there. After I had sourced all the ingredients, I grabbed a couple of packs of some swanky imported beers and put the lot on my card.

When I got home, I laid out all the ingredients and took a photograph of them with my phone before beginning the recipe instructions. I took great care to follow the method precisely: crushing the garlic, grinding the spices, chopping the onions, peeling and de-veining the prawns and mincing the pepper. It was hard work and I wasn't adept at cooking something so complicated. I needed help, so I decided to postpone making the recipe until at least one of the other housemates had returned home. I sat on the kitchen table and waited, briefly wondering if they had even noticed that I had not been around for the last week. I concluded that none of them gave a shit and that I wouldn't have any awkward explaining to do about my previous whereabouts. My presence in that house had been peripheral at best up until that point. But now, things were going to be different. Things were going to change.

*

Thankfully, the first person to come home was Guy. It was exactly who I wanted to see. I wanted to have the opportunity to speak to him privately before I dealt with the others. He was the unspoken leader, after all. Everything went through him.

His face was one of incredulity when he saw me in the kitchen surrounded by quality ingredients from his favourite store and his cookbook open to the Gumbo recipe page.

"Nil? What's all this? Cooking up quite a storm in here, aren't we?" he said as jovially as he could, but I could sense a sneering and suspicious underlying tone. Basically, he didn't trust me, and I knew that was to be expected. We hadn't exactly been compatible up until that point.

I told him that I had decided to make a meal for all the housemates to try and make amends for my previous behaviour. I wanted to start afresh with everyone and show that I could be a part of the group, if they would let me that is. Guy, for once, was taciturn - I could sense that he didn't trust my motives, which was understandable. But, I persisted in order to demonstrate to him that I had changed and was now willing to try and fit in. I told him that I had done some thinking and had realised that I had been a miserable bastard. I made the excuse that I was going through a bad time and needed to adjust. I told him that I appreciated his continued efforts to make me feel part of the group and it was this very persistence that made me realise my worth in the house share. I then went to the fridge and pulled out two ice cold beers, popped the caps and handed one to Guy.

Guy looked at the beer and then back to me before finally reacting with a smile. "Nil, my man. There's no need to apologise! I know how tough it can be trying to adjust to sharing a house with strangers. That's why it is so important to make it as comfortable as possible for everyone. I was just afraid that we had done something to offend you and that's why you were not participating."

I assured Guy that my behaviour was certainly nothing to do with him or the other housemates and that it was all of my own doing. I said that I found it hard to integrate and no-one had ever reached out to me like he had done, so my instinct was to find it threatening. But, now I could see that he had good intentions. I asked him if he would give me another chance, but not only that, I wanted him to help me to see life as he did. I wanted to learn how to experience food and socialising, film and music, parties and going out, relaxing in the sunshine, seeing and doing new things, dancing, drinking, fucking - I wanted to know how it felt to enjoy. Or, more accurately, what it was to enjoy. I said that I had lived my life in the darkness, as an outcast, and he was the only one who could show me the way out.

Guy took a huge gulp of his beer and moved towards me. He embraced me by tightly wrapping one arm around my shoulder and said, "You leave it to me, Nil, you've come to the right person, all I know is how to enjoy my life. It's not what you do that counts. It's how you look at things. It's how you think. It's a state of mind."

He clinked his beer bottle against mine and then took another gulp; I followed suit by taking a swig of my own beer. The beer was bitter and gassy, so I spluttered. Guy laughed at me.

"You'll get the hang of it," he quipped. "Come on, let's get on with this Gumbo. I've been wanting to try this recipe for ages!"

And that was that. Instantly, it was like we were best friends who had known each other for years. That was the way Guy worked. I had always construed this trait of his as insincere, but I was now seeing how comforting it could be if you just accepted it.

He praised me for choosing top-quality ingredients and took a selfie of us standing in front of all of them, instantly posting the photo on a social media site.

Guy followed the recipe with methodical precision, pausing occasionally to record the progress on his phone. He was seemingly a competent chef, but I had no way of knowing whether it just seemed that way or if in fact he really was good at cooking. Every now and then, he would inhale the aroma of the gumbo and exhale approvingly. I was mainly just a spectator in the process, but I willingly performed the small tasks that he assigned me, and I tried to be as positive as I could.

After an hour of tending to the recipe, the others started arriving home. First Loz, then Will and then Oscar. There was no sign of Jana as of yet. They were all initially shocked when they saw me in the kitchen cooking with Guy, and equally surprised when I opened the fridge and handed each of them a beer. None of them asked me where I had been for the last week or even commented on my fat lip, which was all the better for me, as I didn't want to answer those questions. They all praised the aroma in the kitchen and the look of the broth brewing in the pot, stating that they couldn't wait for the meal to be ready. Guy made it clear that it had all been my idea as a way of getting closer to the housemates and that I was the one who had been in charge of cooking the meal – he was merely the assistant. He winked at me and smiled every time he said this.

When the meal was finally ready, we all sat around the kitchen table and Guy gestured for me to be the one to dish the food out. I suggested that we should wait for Jana, but Guy coyly mentioned that she didn't usually join them for dinner and preferred to stay in her room. This made me think that she might have actually been in her room all day, but just didn't want to make her presence known.

As I dished out the portions, everyone swooned and praised me for making such an amazing meal. I felt a sense of pride, even though I had barely been involved with the preparation. Everyone loved the taste of the meal too, or at least pretended that they did.

I listened intently to their conversations over dinner, as I wanted to learn how to converse with them. They mainly engaged in small talk, reminisced about past events that they had experienced together, and name-checked various box sets and bands that led to nods of agreement. The very sound of hearing a particular box set, film, band, or artist being mentioned was enough to create a connection between them. It seemed to be as simple as that: chat about the banal, cite shared past events, reference a cultural focal point, and do not say anything negative - always be positive, no matter what. Easy. So, why was it still so hard for me to get involved?

I was also aware that I was still struggling with my first beer, while the others had all drunk at least two each. Guy noticed this and commented that I needed to "keep up." He went to the fridge and retrieved a beer for me, declaring to the others, "Boys, we are going to need to get Nil drunk tonight!" In response to his proclamation, the others all cheered and banged their bottles on the table.

I took the beer from Guy and chugged it for as long as I could. I heard the others whooping as I did so, but I could only handle it for a few gulps until I spluttered. Guy slapped me on the back. "We'll get you there," he said encouragingly.

When all the beers in the fridge were finished, Guy suggested that we continue the party at the pub. Everyone was fully behind this idea, so we all grabbed our coats and headed out.

On the way there, I felt a slight dizziness - I think the drink was getting to me. I had only had one and a half bottles of beer, but for a non-drinker, that was enough to make me feel half-cut. At first, my natural response to that sensation was to try and fight it and sober myself up. But, on seeing my apprehensiveness, Guy put his arm around my shoulder and assured me that it was fine to feel drunk and that I was among the company of friends who wouldn't let anything bad happen. "Just take it easy," he said. "And don't worry. Enjoy it."

Enjoy it.

Enjoy it.

I had to try to enjoy it, I thought. Therefore, I lowered my guard and decided not to fight the spreading feeling of drunkenness I was experiencing. Tonight would be different from usual, I told myself. Tonight, I would just live in the moment. Tonight, I would be like Guy.

*

The pub was the same one that I had been dragged to on Guy's first night in the house. It was populated by the same drunken patrons, with the same noise and same stale odour that it had exuded before. But, this time, I decided to adjust my filter. I decided not to look at it in the dismissive way that I would usually have done. Maybe, instead of seeing the punters as pathetic booze slaves, I would now try and see them simply as people trying to have a good time. After all, what was wrong with wanting to unwind after a hard day at work and socialise with friends?

I insisted on getting to the bar ahead of the others and being the one to pay for the first round of drinks. They told me the brand names of the beers that they wanted, which I forgot as soon as they told me, so when the bartender finally got round to serving me, I had to ask everyone to repeat their orders. I simply ordered the same thing as Guy did, which was some sort of pilsner. Guy said, "good choice" when he saw me ordering it for myself. I paid for the round with my card and didn't care about the cost.

We took our drinks over to a table and sat down. Before any of us could say anything, Guy held up his glass and made a toast: "I'd just like to thank Nil again for treating us all to a fantastic Gumbo. Great job, mate." Everyone clinked their glasses and said cheers.

The table went quiet for a second, and I felt as though I had been overly quiet in the group thus far, so I took control of the moment and raised my glass so I could also make a toast. I told them how glad I was to have found a house with such amazing people and that I hoped that it would be the start of a lasting friendship. The toast seemed to go down well and eased the tension. Now that the others were more relaxed, the conversation seemed to simply pick up from the one we had been having at the dinner table. I was way out of my depth and knew none of the cultural references that they mentioned. When they asked if I had seen, listened to, heard of, or read any of the things that they were talking about, I simply told them that it was on my list to check out. I tried to make a mental note of all the things they were saying so I could search for them the following day, but there were so many names, titles, places and brands that it was impossible. Furthermore, the more beer I drank, the more my head swirled and I found it hard to focus.

Another round of drinks came and I got up to go to the toilet. My head span as soon as I got off my chair and the whole pub swirled in an obscure reality, like it was some part of a delirious reverie. Guy tapped me on the arm. I looked down at him and he said, "Gents is that way, mate," and pointed in the direction of the toilets. I thanked him and stumbled over to them.

I walked over the piss-sodden tiles of the bathroom to the urinal, but before I could even undo the first button of my jeans, I felt a surge from the pit of my stomach and spontaneously threw up all over the urinal, my shoes and the surrounding floor. All those expensive ingredients that I had bought were now spewing out of my mouth and creating a vile a mess around me. How easily the Gumbo was transformed. As I looked down at the puke with watering eyes, I felt a slap rasp across my back accompanied by a booming laugh. I turned around and saw Guy standing there.

"I thought I'd come and check on you," he said. "I could see that you were looking a bit peaky out there."

I groaned, unable to speak at that point.

"You should feel a bit better after hocking it all up," he continued, as he ushered me over to the sink and helped me wash off the vomit around my mouth. I splashed the cold water over my face and gargled some in my mouth. I looked at myself in the mirror that hung over the sink. I couldn't even recognise my own face; it seemed hazy and distant. I also saw Guy in the mirror standing behind me, but his face seemed clearer than it had ever been. His reflection was almost too clear. It stood out sharp and lucid in a world of distortion.

"It's your first time getting drunk, I'm gathering?" he asked.

I nodded my head.

"Well, there's really no better way to do it. Everyone has to go through this. You drink, you get sick. It gets better though. I guarantee it. Do you think you can carry on?"

I nodded again. Hocking it all up did make me feel better, like Guy had said.

Guy took me back into the pub area and then straight to the bar. He ordered me a shandy - half beer and half lemonade - which was a lot easier to drink. We then went back to join the others.

I sipped the shandy, which was much sweeter-tasting than the pilsner, and tried to find a way into the conversation. They were now talking about Pablo's leaving party, recounting the events and comparing their varying perceptions of the night. I tried to use this conversation to get myself involved. I began to simply recite parts of the party that I remembered - nothing of great amusement, but things that I could remember had happened. These banal memories triggered a positive response in the others; they found my observations amusing and began elaborating on my initial memories. I felt a warm feeling of affirmation that I had never felt before. So, I just continued. I recounted funny incidents from that night as well as things that I had noticed, all the while adding an increasing number of embellishments and exaggerations to make the memories more interesting and funny. Some of the memories that I presented of the night were just outright lies. It didn't matter what was remembered anyway, just *how* we remembered it: accurately or falsely, it was not important.

Later, we made our way home. My head was spinning again and I was finding it hard to make sense of the world around me. My mind was mushy - a dense swirling pool of incoherent nonsense. Guy took me by the arm and guided me home. I just blathered about all kinds of nothing. Mostly, I reiterated various versions of my earlier toast, saying how glad I was to have found that house and how great they all were. I could sense that the others were laughing at me, but my mind was so far removed from the moment that it had no effect on me or my constant drivelling announcements.

When we got back to the house, we sat in Loz's room. They had made a detour to the off-licence on the way home to buy a cheap bottle of tequila, and now Loz was lining up shots for us to down. I necked mine without hesitation and then instantly brought it all back up again in my cupped hands. I ran into the kitchen and continued puking into the sink. It came out thick and fast, sapping me of all energy. I knew the others were next to me, but they sounded like they were in a faraway place. They were either laughing or comforting me, I couldn't be sure.

After all the puke was expelled from my gut, I collapsed on the floor and more or less passed out. In my half-unconscious state, I felt the hands of the others wrap around my body. They carried me up to my room and laid me on my bed. The insects were observing me keenly - they had never seen me in such a state. I cried out for the insects to just fuck off, but maybe the housemates thought it was directed at them. Regardless, they left me on the bed to sleep off the drunkenness.

Soon after, I heard noises from Loz's room as they carried on doing shots, knocking back round after round and playing drinking games. Their laughter and noise was something I had always despised, but now I felt as though I wanted to be down there with them; I felt an intense regret that I was missing out on my chance to integrate and have fun. But, I was in no state to get out of bed. I was in no state for anything except closing my eyes and allowing my body to rid itself of the alcohol poison in my blood. It was self-induced poison that was necessary to aid my transition into the world of enjoyment. I didn't really know what part of that night I enjoyed as I laid there sick and having made a fool of myself, but I knew that I had to do it again the next day.

My eyes felt heavy and I was already dreaming before my eyelids closed. My new life had begun.

*

I awoke the next morning growling. I had a grinding headache and a wet patch around my crotch - I must've pissed myself during the night. My eyes were sore and my mouth was dry and tasted like shit. I got out of bed and took off the previous night's clothes in which I had slept. I wrapped myself in a dressing gown and made my way to the bathroom.

I splashed water on my face and began to remember the details of the previous night. I cringed with embarrassment as I recalled the events and the stupid things that I had said. The memory of the night was blurred and it felt like I had been a character in someone else's dream. I remembered how the others had laughed at my prattling and then how I had puked in front of them all. I wondered if they would ever talk to me again. Could I bear to look them in the eyes?

I had to brush my teeth, as the taste in my mouth was becoming unbearable. But, as soon as the minty flavour of the toothpaste hit my taste buds, it triggered the remnants of my stomach contents from the previous night to be ejected through my mouth. That gumbo was determined to get itself out of me completely.

I got into the shower and cleaned myself thoroughly, attempting to brush my teeth again while letting the jets of water splash into my mouth. This time, I managed to clean my teeth without heaving.

After the shower, I went back to my room, changed the bed sheets and got dressed in clean clothes. I could hear from downstairs that some of the others were in the kitchen. I briefly thought about just staying in my room and avoiding any confrontation, and although I knew that to be the easy option, I also knew it would be the worst thing to do. I had to go and apologise for the previous night, so I went downstairs and into the kitchen with my head hung and an apology ready. But, before I could say a thing, they all greeted me with a loud cheer.

"Hey, Nil! Glad you're back in the world of the living! You seriously zombied out on us last night," Guy said and then proceeded to mimic a zombie walking around in a mindless state. The others laughed. Guy stopped his impression and came up to me, patting me lightly on the back. "Only joking, my man. We're glad you loosened up last night. It was good to see the real you."

The real me?

Guy handed me a freshly made cup of tea. "Here you go. You deserve this. I just made it for myself, but I think you could use it more than me. I'll make myself another one," he said.

I thanked him and sat down at the kitchen table where Loz and Will were sitting. I told them, making sure Guy could also hear, that I was really sorry about my behaviour last night. They said that there was nothing to apologise for and that it was the best that they had seen from me the whole time that I had been in the house. I told them that I was at least sorry for puking everywhere and that I wanted to make it up to them. It must have been horrible for them, having to clean it up.

Guy brought his new cup of tea over to the table and sat down. He looked at me gravely and said, "What you did. You'll never be able to make it up to us…" He paused for dramatic effect and then stared deeply into my eyes, seemingly scrutinising my very being. He held his unwavering expression for at least five seconds before creasing up with laughter. "I'm only joking, dude. I tell you what, you can buy us all a beer over at the Fields today? Make it up to us that way."

I was confused. What fields did he mean?

"We're all going over to London Fields later," he clarified. "Have you seen the weather outside? Glory days! We're going to get some beers, maybe a disposable barbecue, and just enjoy the rays!"

I said that I couldn't possibly drink anything today given how sick I was feeling.

"The only way to cure a hangover is more alcohol. Hair of the dog! We're leaving in an hour, so be ready," he stated, leaving no room for objection or refusal.

An hour later, all the housemates, except for Jana, were in the kitchen ready to leave. They all had their summer clothes on; shorts, flip-flops, straw hats and sunglasses. I wore full-length jeans, boots and a t-shirt. It was the most summery outfit that I could find. We left the house and had to get two different buses en route. The buses were hot, cramped and took an age to get there.

By the time we arrived at London Fields, which was a city park largely covered with grass, it was heaving with people doing exactly what we planned to do. Everyone was splayed out on the grass just chatting, drinking and sunbathing. It was like a music festival, without the music. They all sat in circles in their own little cliques and performed to each other in various ways. I even saw one young woman parading around with her bare breasts out, which was something that you didn't often see in English parks.

We crossed the park, weaving in and out of the people on the floor. We were all just following Guy as he searched for the perfect spot. He finally settled on a patch of grass that had just been vacated by another group. It was right amongst the action.

On one side of us there was a group passing around a huge joint while taking zero notice of their friend who was passionately serenading them with his guitar. On the other side to us there were a group of young women working on their tans. Their bare, bronzed skin glistening in the sunlight as precious as gold. The sight of the young women aroused a yearning in me; I wanted to know what it was like to feel their supple shimmering bodies.

We all sat on the floor and unpacked our beers and food. Someone had also bought a few bags of ice to try and keep the beers cold in the increasing heat. I was burning up in my jeans and boots and envied all the others in the park, who were sporting their relaxed summer wear.

The others cracked open their beers, so I followed suit. I drew the can to my mouth, but pulled it away when I smelt the beer inside. It instantly made me want to wretch. The sickness returned - my body's way of warning me not to poison it like I had done the previous night. I looked over at Guy and saw that he was monitoring me. He nodded as a way of telling me that I had to drink the beer. I gulped to prepare my throat and then drew the can to my lips, quickly downing a mouthful of the vile liquid. It tasted even worse than it had done the previous night, and I had to struggle not to instantly puke it all back up again. That first sip was the worst, yet the more I drank of the can, the more I got used to it. Also, Guy was right, it calmed my hangover somewhat. I started to relax.

I laid back down on the grass and turned my head to look at the bare skin of the sunbathers next to me, allowing the heat of the sun to wash over my body. My brow began to sweat and my skin redden, but instead of becoming agitated by the heat, I let it consume and relax me, like the sunbathers were doing.

I began to drift off under the radiating sun to the vision of a vast field the colour and texture of bare and soft female skin, and just as I was about to jump into the pool of flesh, I heard "Nil!" It was Guy calling my name. I opened my eyes. "Don't pass out on us again. Here, have another beer, bro."

I rubbed my eyes and sat up. Guy handed me another can of beer from the bag of ice and leaned into me. "You like those girls, huh?" he whispered into my ear. "Fucking hot, right?"

I emitted a nervous giggle and nodded.

"You wanna go and talk to them?" He said.

I shook my head and said that I couldn't possibly disturb them while they were laid out like that.

"There's never a better time do it than the present. If you wait, then they might leave. Or worse yet, be picked up by some other men. There's a lot on the prowl around here."

I looked around the park and couldn't see any such activity going on. Everyone seemed to be engrossed in their own little groups. I told Guy that I didn't see it.

"You're not looking hard enough," he scoffed. "Come on, go and talk to them."

I shook my head vigorously.

"Ok, you'll regret that. Live in the moment, man. Carpe Diem!"

And with that, he stood up and went over to the sunbathers to wake them out of their slumber. I couldn't hear what he was saying, but within seconds, they were all sitting up paying attention to his words. He was sat cross-legged amongst them and they laughed and responded to everything he said. What words could he possibly be using? Surely no words were that potent. Or, was it just his self-confidence that they were responding to? Needless to say, I was in awe as I watched Guy talk to them; it reminded me of how he had won over Jana at the skating rink. He did it so effortlessly, luring them into his narrative and making it suit his desires. What came so easily to him, was excruciatingly difficult for me. Will, Oscar and Loz were chatting amongst themselves and paying no attention to Guy's pursuits. This led me to surmise that this must be a regular occurrence.

After about five minutes, Guy stood up and the sunbathers joined him. He brought them over to where we were sitting. My heart began to pound out of my body. We all looked at the young women and they all looked at us, but before any kind of silence could brew, Guy spoke.

"This is Loz, Will, Oscar and Nil," he said to the young women. "And this is Lorna, Kristine and Maria. They're from Denmark," he said to us and winked.

They all sat down with us and Guy offered them each a beer from the ice bag, which was rapidly becoming a bag of water.

I remained quiet as they all partook in small talk about their trip to London. How long are you here for? What do you think of it so far? Where are you staying? What are you studying? Oh, that's interesting, I studied that too! Where else have you been this summer?

When the small talk was exhausted, Guy jumped in and began telling stories of our group's antics. He recalled how I was drunk the previous night and puked after a shot of tequila. The Danes laughed and I could feel myself blushing. I thought I caught Kristine's gaze for a second, and I wondered if that meant she liked me. I couldn't read signals very well. I had trouble understanding the subtleties of human expression. I decided to test the waters, so I regaled them with more details of my drunken night. I joked that it was the most that I had ever spent on ingredients for a meal and I ended up puking it all over my feet. They laughed. Guy beamed at me with approval.

After a while, the Danes said that they needed to leave, but would try and catch up with us that evening if we went to a bar. Everyone swapped numbers and made sure we could stay in contact. As they left, I again caught Kristine glancing in my direction.

When they were out of sight, we all relaxed and started raving and getting excited about them, discussing how good-looking they were. Will mentioned that he thought Kristine was looking at him, which made me angry at him or her or myself - I'm not sure which.

It was still early afternoon, so we still had a lot of the day to kill. We drank some more, played frisbee and then got the barbecue going. The barbecue attracted the attention of the marijuana-smoking group next to us, who we ended up sitting with and trading chicken legs for drags on their joints. I refrained from smoking though. I was already struggling to handle the alcohol, so mixing it with marijuana would just be too much, too soon.

We continued in that vein as the afternoon wore on and turned into evening. As the sun began to set, we all decided to keep the party going. The marijuana group knew of an event that was happening nearby, which apparently was going to be "sick". We decided to join them.

We all got up to leave. Although there weren't many people left in the park, the traces of the day's festivities were everywhere. The place was strewn with beer cans, cigarette butts and empty food packets. There were also a number burnt out patches on the grass; evidence of where the barbecues had been. The excess of human indulgence lay on the ground as if it was meant as a symbol of pride. Look how much fun we had!

The park may have been emptying out, but the surrounding bars and pubs were now filling up. It seemed that the fun was not to be over yet.

*

We navigated our way through the backstreets until we found ourselves at a rundown warehouse. By this time, I was already feeling drunk and wasn't sure how much more alcohol I could consume. All the others had drunk considerably more than I had - probably three or four times as much - but they were all used to it and I was not. I couldn't understand how they could chug beer after beer and still seem to retain a modicum of soberness about them. I tried my utmost to conceal drunken feelings, which was a difficult task - my legs began to feel too weak to carry my body.

We stood outside the warehouse while one of the men from the marijuana group negotiated with the doorman. It was a relaxed security affair, but marijuana man wanted to get us all in for free, as he knew the promoter or something. The doorman said that there were too many of us to get in for free, but he would let us in for a discounted price, to which we agreed.

There was a carpark outside the warehouse that served as a smoking area and a place for people to chat. Inside was where the main action was taking place. It wasn't full by any means, but it was filling up. Apparently, we had arrived very early, even though I noted to myself that I would usually have been in bed by that time.

There was a band playing on a makeshift stage and a small crowded bar area that was serving drinks. Basic drinks though: beer from cans, spirits and mixers, and wine - red or white. I didn't bother going to get a drink, blaming the size of the crowd at the bar. However, Guy expertly fought his way through and promptly brought me back a beer. He told me that I should keep on drinking otherwise I'd start to flag.

I cracked open the can of beer and watched the band for a bit before changing my focus to the crowd and then to the members of our group. The marijuana set had broken off and were doing their own thing now, while Guy, Will, Oscar and Loz nodded their heads to the music. Guy leaned into me and said something, but I couldn't hear what he said as the volume was way too loud. I asked him to repeat it, which he did, but I still couldn't hear. He then put his mouth right into my earhole.

"What do you think of the band?!" He shouted.

I said that they were very good.

To be honest, I had no idea what I thought of the band. It was cranked up so loud that it all just sounded like a muffled mess. Also, I had nothing to compare it to; I didn't have any knowledge of music or pop culture, so I didn't know how they compared to other bands of that ilk. But, I didn't dwell on that too long; instead, I began to nod my head to the beat to show my appreciation. Each song sounded like the last, but I continued to nod my head like the others were doing. The band's set seemed to drag on for ages and my legs grew tired, although that didn't seem to concern the others who were watching on and enjoying the show.

Finally, after the band had finished, we all went out into the carpark. Guy was out of beer and told me that it was my turn to buy a round. So, I made my way back into the warehouse to fight and jostle with the throng in order to get served. I was being poked, elbowed and shoved all over the place. It reminded me of that packed bus that I had taken. A single human entity that was at odds with itself.

After much vying, I managed to get two cans of beer and I took them outside and gave one to Guy. The mood had flattened amongst the group and there wasn't much conversation. They were just looking around as if trying to find something to do. I could see that Guy's agitation was increasing due to the lack of exuberance. He jolted himself out of the lull, "Come on," he said, "Let's get in there and dance!"

He strode back into the warehouse and we all followed behind; it wasn't long before Guy had them all dancing to the music, which was now being peddled by a DJ. I didn't join in with them at first. Even though I was completely drunk by that point, I still didn't have the urge to dance. I simply didn't know what to do. There were many people on the dance floor now and they were all dancing quite violently in their own way. There seemed to be no thought or consideration shown to the people around them. It was simply about their own pleasure.

Guy came over and said, "Come on Nil. Get involved!"

I told him that I didn't know how to dance.

"It's easy," he said. "You just move your arms and legs about a bit. Let the vibrations flow through you and try to feel one with the music. I mean listen to those beats, it's heaven itself!"

I said that I didn't want to look like a fool.

"A fool? Who cares what people think? Dance like no-one's watching!"

Dance like no-one's watching. I had always despised that saying, but now I thought I would see what would happen if I embraced it. I was sufficiently drunk enough by that point not to care anyway. So, I just let loose. I closed my eyes so I couldn't see the other people and then I just flung my arms out and moved my feet on the dance floor like no-one was watching. What a sight it must've been as I span around, flapping my arms and bobbing my head. I felt myself bump into a few people, but I treated it like all the other dancers - if they were unfortunate enough to get in the way of my good time, then so be it.

I danced like that for around five songs, all the while my mind blank and thinking of nothing. I imagined that when I opened my eyes, I would be the centre of attention with everyone standing around me looking and laughing at the sight. But, I was wrong. When I opened my eyes, I saw that no-one was taking any notice of me at all. There was no laughing or derision directed towards my dancing. Everyone was still dancing and acting like they had been before, all too encapsulated in their own personal reveries to care about what I was doing.

I made my way to the toilet, waited patiently in the long, long line and when I eventually got into a cubicle I threw up everywhere. I went to the sink and swigged some water around in my mouth before heading back to the dance floor. I didn't mention to anyone that I had puked again and just got back to dancing and tried to feel this "oneness" with the music. Maybe I just needed to hear more of it so I could get used to it.

Later, we bumped into the marijuana group again who told us that they were leaving and going back to their flat for an afterparty. They asked if we were up for it and Guy said "Yes." His phone beeped and he looked at the screen - it was a message from the sunbathing Danes. He messaged back, telling them to come to the afterparty.

It was around two in the morning at that point and we had been out for over twelve hours straight. I fought hard against the tiredness and followed them all through the streets. The marijuana group had picked up more people from the warehouse, so there were now about fifteen of us in the group.

We made it to a tiny flat and all crammed into the living room. One of them rolled a joint, while another put on some music. Everyone else was talking and drinking amongst themselves. I just wanted to fall asleep right where I was. Guy was still as energised as ever though and became even more excited when he received another text from the Danes. He left the room and when he returned, he had the three young women in tow. They looked drunk and red-eyed, just like the rest of us in that room. I was sure that Kristine glanced over at me, but Will nudged me in the side and whispered in my ear that she had just looked at him again. I was sure that he was wrong.

Even though the flat was tiny, everyone still managed to break off into their own little groups and talked amongst themselves. I was pushed to the fringes, but tried to stay on the inside track with the Danes. It was hard though, as Will and Guy took control of the situation. I ended up in the splinter group with Loz and Oscar who looked as if they were ready to close their eyes and sleep for a thousand years.

The joint that one of them had rolled earlier made its way to me. I felt the room fix their eyes upon me to make sure I actually smoked it. I reluctantly put it to my mouth and took a few drags. My head instantly spun and I felt that another puking session was imminent. I passed the joint on to the next person and I excused myself from the room as casually as I could. For all they knew, I was simply going for a piss.

In the bathroom, I bent over the toilet bowl and threw up three times, washed my mouth out and then went back into the living room. I came back to see Will necking with Kristine. It seemed that she had been looking at him all along.

I found a comfortable spot on the sofa and lent my head to the side. I could feel sleep dragging me under. It was impossible to resist.

I closed my eyes to the spinning world. A world that taunted me with enjoyment but so far had failed to deliver. A world where Will had his tongue in Kristine's mouth. A world that was red-eyed and intoxicated. A world that belonged to Guy.

A world that I wished belonged to me.

*

The world was still spinning when I awoke the next day. My head ached and my eyes were blurred. It took a good thirty seconds for my vision to return to me, and when it did, I saw that I was still in the same position on that sofa. There was a long string of saliva hanging out of my mouth. I wiped it away with the inside of my T-shirt and looked around to see if I could find anyone familiar. Guy, Will, Oscar and Loz were all gone and so were the Danes. However, there were still four revellers from the previous night laid out asleep on the floor, and there was even someone curled up next to me on the sofa. She was snoring loudly through her wide open mouth. I slowly pulled myself off the sofa, being careful not to wake her, and crept over the bodies lying on the floor.

I left the flat and stood on the street. It was a lot colder than the previous day with a overcast black cloud covering the sky, and it was drizzling with rain. I also had no idea where I was. The area was unfamiliar and far away from my house. I pulled out my phone to search for my location on the maps app, but my phone was out of battery. I considered going back into the flat to ask for directions or at least ask where I was, but I didn't know any of their names and couldn't even remember the number of the flat or which floor it was on.

I walked the streets, trying to find a Tube or train station or even a bus stop to figure out where I was. All I wanted was to be at home and crawl into bed. I was sick with a hangover, I was tired and my muscles ached from sleeping in an awkward position on that sofa. I found a bus stop, but none of it made any sense. I still didn't understand what part of London I was in. East somewhere. That's all I knew.

I entered a newsagent and asked where the nearest train or Tube station was and the employee pointed me in the direction of some Overground station that I had never heard of before. I searched around for it, asking various people for directions on the way. Finally, I found it.

I topped up ten pounds on my Oyster using my bank card. A shiver spiked through my body. I dreaded to think how much money I had remaining in my bank account. I did some mental arithmetic and calculated that after the next month's rent came out, I would be very close to or would already have sunk into my overdraft.

I waited for the train in the wet, cold weather and wondered what I was going to do for money. My overdraft was five hundred pounds, so I knew that would keep me going, but only as a temporary measure.

The train arrived and I embarked with the few other early-morning Sunday passengers. The train rattled along and I tried hard not to puke. I managed to hold it in for the length of the train ride, but threw up on the platform after I disembarked. An older woman glared at me in disgust.

That was only the beginning of the journey. From there, I got on another train and then a bus in order to make it home. It was torture.

It was still morning when I arrived and the house was quiet. I wondered if Will was in his room with Kristine and whether Guy was in his room with the other two - maybe they had all gone back to the Danes' hotel.

I shuffled upstairs, looking forward to climbing into bed and as I opened my door, I heard the bathroom door open at the same time. I looked around and I saw Jana emerging, fresh from taking a shower and wrapped in a thick dressing gown. We briefly caught each other's gaze but she quickly looked away, hurrying into her room.

As soon as I was safe in the confines of my own room, I ripped off my clothes, climbed into bed and pulled the warm blanket over me. The insects were watching. I closed my eyes and dreamt of everything and nothing.

Later, I was awoken by a knock on my door. I got out of bed, quickly pulled on some clothes and opened the door - it was Guy. He looked pleased to see me.

"Great! You made it home, I see. I tried calling you, but I couldn't get through," he said.

I told him that my phone's battery had died.

"I'm sorry that we left you there," he went on. "We tried waking you, but you were out for the count. I shook you and shouted in your ear, but nothing! In the end, we thought it just better to leave you."

I told him not to worry.

He came into my room and sat down on my bed. He looked uneasily at the insects on my shelves before turning his attention to his phone.

"I've got some of the tracks from that band that were playing yesterday. You said you liked them, right?" he said, scrolling through his phone.

I told him that I thought they were good.

"Cool. I've just sent you the tracks and also a couple of the others that you were dancing to afterwards."

I couldn't even remember the songs I was dancing to, and it took me a few seconds to even remember that I had danced at all. I then asked him the question that had been on my mind all morning. I asked him what had happened with the Danes.

"Oh, yeah," he smirked. "We had some fun. Will too." And that was that; it was all he was going to say on the subject.

He began to play a track from his phone and told me that it was by a band that was similar to one that played last night. We listened in silence. I wasn't sure what he wanted me to say as we listened to it, so I just lightly bobbed my head to the beat to show my appreciation. When it had finished. I told him that it was a good one.

"I'll send you that one too then," he said.

As he began searching through his phone again, I quickly asked him how Jana was doing. I tried to make the question seem as casual as possible, but he could see right through my attempt. He put his phone down and looked straight at me with a grimace.

"Forget about Jana," he told me. "She's a strange girl. Never comes out of her room and barely talks. After that night at the skating rink, she kind of retreated back into her shell."

This brought up so many other questions in my head, but before I could form any of them into speech, Guy got up off the bed and put his hand on my shoulder.

"Trust me, she ain't worth it, mate. There are so many other girls out there for you. Get a dating app or go out to a bar or a cafe. They're everywhere. Just have confidence in yourself. That's all they look for. Confidence." He pondered for a second. "I tell you what.

I'll take you out on Friday. Just me and you. I'll show you how it's done."

I thanked him but told him that I was running low on money now and I doubted I would be able to go out again. He asked me what happened to my job and I said that I had been fired.

"Did you enjoy it there?" he asked and I said no. "They did you a favour, then," he replied boldly. "You need to find a job you love. That you adore. Look at me. I love my job. I can't wait to get in and do it every Monday. I wouldn't do it otherwise, I'd just leave. A job has to match your dreams and ambitions. It has to be your hobby and make you feel like you are contributing something wonderful to the world. It has to be an extension of who you are, of what you love."

I asked him what he did and he gave me a job-title that I didn't even understand, but I got the gist that he worked in marketing or media, in an advertising company or something. He told me that they gave him promotions all the time and that he was starting to make a lot of money, or "big bucks" as he called it.

I squirmed when he told me all of this. Where was I to find a job that I loved, or even liked, and also one that I could make money from? Was enjoying your job truly an option for everyone?

"If you need some money to get by I can lend you some," he said casually. "I'm starting to get so much coming in that I don't know what to do with it all."

I thanked him and said that I would use that as the last option, as I didn't want to start being in debt.

"Well, there is another way," he said as he picked up the *Lucanus cervus* and inspected it closely. "I bet some of these insect things are worth money."

I told him that although the one he was studying wasn't worth anything, some of them were rare pieces and could sell for hundreds of pounds.

"There you go then! Sell some of these off. And, I mean not just for the money either. You should sell them because they're creepy."

I didn't say anything back.

"Nil. You came to me and asked me how to start a new life. One where you enjoyed things and fit in. You should start that life by getting rid of these things. They do you no favours. Say you bring a girl back and she sees all this shit! She'll be off and out of here within seconds! Fitting in should become your whole life, from your room, to your possessions, to your clothes, to your job, to the way you talk, to the way you look at things. You need to decide who you want to be as an individual and work at it. Shape your individuality into a recognisable mould that people can understand and latch on to. What's your lifestyle going to be? What's your niche? All this insect shit doesn't fit in anywhere. Be an individual. Don't be a weirdo."

I nodded and Guy got off the bed and headed for the door.

"So, we're set for Friday then?" he asked, waiting for me to give him the correct answer.

I told him that Friday worked for me.

"Good. That will give you time to sort this room out and maybe think about getting some decent clothes." He opened the door, got halfway out, then turned back and said, "Live your dreams," and then closed the door behind him.

Live your dreams. Live like there's no tomorrow. Do what you love. Dance like no one's watching. Be an individual.

I sat back on my bed and tried to clear my head. If there's one thing indulging in culture requires, it's money - a lot of money. Whether it's subversive, mainstream, underground or the everyday, it all costs money. I knew what my next step had to be now, so I opened my computer and began searching for sites where I could sell off my insects. I needed to make some money before Friday.

*

I put my insects up for sale and almost instantly got an order for the entire collection. They all went to one collector. I agreed to a price with him; it was below the price that I wanted, but seeing how he was buying the lot, I didn't mind.

I packed each insect carefully with bubble wrap, put them all in one big box and sent them to their new owner.

My room felt empty without their hollow gaze so I decided to reinvigorate my room like Guy had suggested. I didn't want to spend too much money on it, but just enough to make a difference. I changed the dark black fabric curtains to a neat wooden Venetian blind. I threw out the old frayed bed sheets and replaced them with new ones that had pastel shades. I laid a circular mat with a geometric pattern design next to my bed to cover the worn carpet and I cleaned the sash window until it gleamed. I left the shelves mostly empty apart from a speaker dock for my phone where I could play music, and a funky analogue clock that I bought at the vintage furniture shop that Guy had once recommended to Jana. And finally, I threw away all my insect books and journals. I took one last look through "Social Insects: Ecology and Behavioural Biology" by M.V. Brian and then threw them all in the bin.

After I had finished, I stood back and admired the room. It was bright, airy and clean. I showed Guy and he approved, saying that the final touch would be to add some of my own personality. He suggested a stack of art books, a vinyl collection, or a display of vintage beer bottles. But, he said not to worry too much about that yet and at least I was rid of those "creepy insects". I just needed to replace them with another collection, but one that was not compulsive or weird.

After he left my room, I sat on my bed and played the music Guy had given me on my new speaker dock. I listened to the music carefully, learning the beats and the melodies of the music and trying to decipher what part of it was meant to speak to me, what part I was meant to feel the oneness with, and where my spine was meant to tingle. I guessed that I was supposed to feel melancholic when there was a minor note, euphoric after a succession of major chords or a key change, inspired at a crescendo, reflective with a slow tempo, invigorated with a fast tempo. The code was all hidden in the musical arrangement, I just needed to adjust my sensory reflexes accordingly to *feel* it. If I knew the structural and mechanistic cues that prompted people to feel a certain way, then I could emulate that and learn how to do it for myself.

While I was listening to the music I used the time to search the internet for a new job. The money from the sale of the insects would only last for a limited time and I needed something more long term. I tried to follow Guy's advice and look for something that I would enjoy, but there were zero jobs that fit that description. I would have to figure out what kind of work that I actually enjoyed first. I decided that the best way to go about it was to simply copy the job that Guy was doing. I knew that I wouldn't be able to instantly get a position as high up as Guy, but I could start at the bottom in that profession, with a view to working my way up the ladder. I searched for all the marketing jobs I could find at entry level and applied to them all. I applied for them regardless of whether they needed experience or certain qualifications. Throw enough shit at the fan…

I also went to temp agencies, but I wasn't wearing the appropriate clothing to ask for an office job. They had me pegged as a warehouse type as soon as they saw me. I didn't even own a proper buttoned shirt - I had never had the need. I knew that I would have to also get some new clothes like Guy had also suggested.

Meanwhile, I had also signed up to a few streaming sites and began the task of watching all the programs that the housemates had discussed in the pub the other day. There were so many to choose from and each programme had countless episodes attached, all lasting forty-five minutes to an hour each. I decided the best way was to just dive in and try to ingest as much information as I could. Try to learn the plots and the character names and even figure out the sub-text. Again, just like the music, the code to these programs was all in the structure and style. It was just a case of working out the mechanics. I read some information on story structure and character development on the internet and I soon thought I had it all worked out. I listened carefully to the scores and studied the camera shots, realising that these cues were also a guide to what genre the program was and how you should feel when watching. Also, I read some blogs and forums and learnt the plot twists and story developments that people thought were particularly impactful or weak and watched the programs bearing this in mind. I wanted to learn how others felt or reacted so I could try to feel and react in the same way. I knew that the enjoyment of culture would come. I just had to stick with it. Learn it. Become it.

When I thought that I had stuffed enough information into my brain to have a conversation with the housemates, I went into the kitchen at a time when they were all convening and tried to put my knowledge into action. I regurgitated all the reference points, character names, band names, lyrics, plot twists, vocal hooks that I had memorised over the course of the week and then we sat down to eat spaghetti carbonara.

*

Friday soon came and by that time, I had engorged myself on all the culture that I could fit in.
I had visited an art gallery on Tuesday and had studied all the modern art that was on display. Later in the evening, I had watched clip after clip of viral videos online. On Wednesday, I went to the cinema and watched a new blockbuster film. After, I went to a new bespoke burger place that Guy and Loz had recommended. In the evening, I researched places to go travelling while continuing to watch more and more of the programs that everyone had told me were a "must see". On Thursday there was an exhibition of an old pop singer's clothes and guitars along with various memorabilia. Everyone told me it was a "must visit", so I went. I listened to one of his albums on the way there. After that, I watched some more TV shows on my computer and also created a social media account and saw what everyone had to say.
I had consumed excessively and it had left me exhausted and confused. I had not known where to start, so I just drank it all in as one big gulp. All the information was just spinning through my head, creating a dizzying feeling of weightless unreality. It was a constant bombardment of images and propaganda, telling us what we need, want and desire. The advertisements for how to live were

woven inside everything, not just products and companies, but art and film and music too. The adverts were just like the insects, staring at me with dead eyes, unsure whether I was being judged or just observed. But, I knew that they were there, staring right through me. When I looked at them, they looked back, only with greater intensity.

Despite all this, I was still looking forward to the night out with Guy. I had seen so many young women from my indulgence in culture that it was fuelling an irrepressible sexual appetite. Usually, I would keep to my room and only go out when necessary, and when I was out, I would keep my head down. Now I had opened myself up to society, I saw women everywhere and wanted to know more than anything what it felt like to be with one. I had even begun to watch some porn online. And, the more I watched, the more I got used to its depravity. There was so much to choose from - an incomprehensible amount. I couldn't believe that there were so many people in the world willing to partake in it, and some of it was truly demeaning too. I really hoped that Guy would stay true to his word and help me talk to women that night. So, it was annoying when he said that the plans had changed and all the housemates now also wanted to come out with us. However, Guy assured me that he was going to concentrate his efforts on helping me to talk to the opposite sex. I was a bit apprehensive about putting myself out like that in front of the others, but there was no choice but to just go along with the plan. I mentioned to Guy that I couldn't afford to buy any new clothes and didn't even know what I was looking for, even if I did have the money. He grimaced and told me he would try to help me out. At first, he rooted through his clothes to see if there was anything he could lend me, but he was much taller and more muscular, so all his clothes just hung off my pathetic frame - it was almost as if his clothes were mocking me. He gave up on that idea and instead, chose to root through my cupboards to see if he could find anything salvageable. He found nothing. Ultimately, he borrowed a pair of jeans from Loz and a top from Will to dress me. My shoes were still a problem, but luckily, Guy's feet were only one size larger than mine so I borrowed a pair from him. I felt like a fucking clown in those clothes, but Guy assured me that I looked good, so I just accepted it.

After my humiliating makeup session was over, we ordered a takeaway from a nearby restaurant and ate it in the kitchen. The food was Moroccan, which they insisted on telling me. While we were eating, Jana came through the front door with some shopping. She looked at us and I think she contemplated just taking it all upstairs to her room, but as we had already clocked her, she knew that it was out of the question. So, she brought the shopping into the kitchen and began putting it away. Guy looked at her uneasily and I could sense the tension, but as usual, he just couldn't bear there being an awkward silence and informed her that we were all going out. She nodded. There was then another silence and I thought that I would test the waters, so I asked

Jana if she wanted to join us. The other housemates remained quiet. Jana just continued to put her shopping away, while Guy interjected and said, "I don't think she'll want to come. It's not really her kind of thing."

Jana turned, looked at me and purely out of spite for Guy's comment, told me that she'd love to come along and that she would go and get ready. Guy simply said, "Great news."

I knew that there was tension between the two, but I really did want Jana to come along.

After she left the kitchen to go and get ready, the conversation switched back to normal instantly. I was half waiting for Guy to scold me for asking her to come, but he didn't. He just carried on as usual without treating it as a big deal. They talked for a while about one of the programs I had been trying to catch up on. They had reached a far later season, but at least I knew who the characters were and what the general premise was. I was just about able to contribute on some kind of level. They were impressed by my knowledge of the program and responded positively to my input. They then reminded me that the food was Moroccan barbecue.

*

Jana didn't take long to get ready. In fact, she was ready within ten minutes. She came into the kitchen and sat next to me. I offered her a beer and to my surprise, she took one.

Soon, we were on the Tube making our way to the bar. Guy assured us that it was a hip place that hadn't been "discovered" yet. I sat beside Jana and she stayed next to me the whole time, seemingly not wanting to converse with the others unless absolutely necessary. I didn't mind; in fact, I liked it. We didn't actually talk to each other too much, but we were comfortable sitting in silence. When we spoke, it was just functional with no small talk or trivialities. Talking and being with her was the antithesis of talking and being with the other housemates.

When we arrived at the bar and ordered some drinks, Guy pulled me aside. "Nil, look at all the action in here. There are loads of hot girls. Are we going to do this or not?" he said.

I told him I was up for it, even though I felt bad for leaving Jana talking with the others. I looked around to see if I could see her, but she was out of sight. I didn't know whether she was in the toilet or had gone home.

Guy didn't wait - he was already talking to a pair of young women by the time I had turned back around. One of them was gorgeous and the other was average. Guy was putting all his effort into the gorgeous one, so I guessed he had left the average one for me to talk to. I didn't have any idea what to say to her, but luckily enough, she started the conversation and it just continued from there. Where are you from? What do you do? What do you eat? Where do you go? What do you listen to? What do you watch? Who are you? What are you? Where are we?

Through a combination of citing the references that I had learnt over the past few days and outright lying, I think I managed to converse adequately with her. Also, Guy was right next to me, and he was pitching in and making jokes whenever he saw that I was struggling. It felt like I had been talking to her for hours, but when I glanced at the time on my phone, I saw that it had been less than ten minutes.

The gorgeous one suggested that we go outside for a cigarette, so that's what we all did. Except, they weren't real cigarettes, they were e-cigarettes. The average one mentioned that she could enjoy smoking them so much more knowing that they weren't doing the damage of a regular cigarette. I agreed, not knowing what the hell she was talking about. I took a few puffs on the e-cigarette and told them that it was just as good as smoking a normal cigarette.

I noticed that both of them had a copious amount of tattoos, so I brought it up as a conversation. They asked us if we had any, of course Guy did, and also had a heartfelt or funny anecdote for each one. I told them that I didn't have any yet but it was definitely in the pipeline. I picked a particularly extravagant tattoo on the average one's arm and asked her where she got it done. I told her that I would check out that place when I get mine done.

Guy looked at me proudly - I was catching on.

When they had excused themselves to go to the toilet, Guy grabbed me by the shoulders and shook me. "You're doing it, man! I knew you had it in you!" he said.

I smiled and asked him if I really had a chance.

"A chance?" he said, "You're a dead cert! Just keep it up and don't let the conversation flatten. And don't worry, I'll be the one to seal the deal and get them back to the house, so you don't have to panic."

I thanked him, then paused. I asked him about Jana, saying that it seemed like I might have a chance with her, as she had stayed close to me on the Tube on the way there. Guy screwed up his face.

"Well, where is she now? I don't see her. I'm not being horrible, but you don't stand a chance with her. She's an odd cunt. What you need is a one night stand, just to get that monkey off your back. Am I right?"

I nodded.

"This one here is on. There is no chance I'll let it fail. If you go for Jana, you'll just end up disappointed. You'll get nothing. I guarantee you'll get sex if you stay on course. OK?"

I nodded again and told him that he was certainly right. I excused myself to go to the toilet and he told me to bring some drinks back. I agreed and went off to the toilet.

I took a long piss and thought about what Guy had said, agreeing with myself that he was right. I needed to just go along with it now, it was why I had wanted to go out in the first place. Anyway, I didn't even know if Jana was still there, she had probably gone home already.

I came out of the toilet and headed for the bar to get a round of drinks and saw Jana sitting on a table on her own, nursing a bottle of beer. I contemplated just walking right past and ignoring her, but I just couldn't do that. I sat down next to her and asked where the others were and she said she didn't know. She asked me where I had been and I told her I was talking with Guy. Silence ensued. There were so many things that I wanted to ask her, but one question in particular was stuck in my mind. It was the one question that had been tormenting me since the night I left the house and went to sleep on the streets. But, I couldn't ask her - it was too personal. I fidgeted on the seat and then, as if she was reading my mind, she said,

"You want to know why I slept with Guy, don't you?" Her voice was clear and precise and cut through all the noise that was permeating throughout the bar.

I looked down at the table and didn't answer. I wanted to tell her that it was the only thing I had been able to think about since it had happened, but I couldn't.

"Well," she continued, "I don't know if you want to know, but I want to tell you. I need to tell you. Do you ever just do something, go along with something because you feel that you have to? That there is some sort of external pressure that makes you think it is the right thing to do, even though you know it's wrong? Guy was that person. The one that you feel you must like and be like - the one that I felt I should be with. When it was over, I was sickened with myself. But, there was just this pressure, this strange invisible pressure, almost as if it was guiding my actions with the promise of some sort of fulfilment, like if I went through with it. I don't know, I..." She trailed off, unsure how to finalise her thoughts.

Then, she looked straight at me. "Do you know what I mean?" she asked, craving validation.

I looked her straight in the eyes and then spouted some trivial bullshit about how she should not beat herself up about it or something. I excused myself and said that I needed to bring Guy a beer as he was waiting for me. I just left her alone, nursing her beer and feeling completely exposed.

I went to the bar, ordered a round, and took the drinks back outside to Guy and the two young women.

I pretended to be listening as the average one told me about her job, but really, I was thinking about Jana and what she had said to me. I had known exactly what Jana meant and I couldn't fathom why I hadn't responded to her. I had just given away the opportunity to connect with someone who felt the same way as I did. An opportunity like that had never come up before in my life and I just ignored it like I didn't know what she was talking about. I thought about her sitting alone at that table, feeling embarrassed that she had just opened herself up only to be shut off. A feeling of guilt consumed my body. I looked at the average one to whom I was talking and wondered why I had listened to Guy, relinquishing my opportunity to connect with Jana for this.

I excused myself to go to the toilet to see if I could go back and find Jana to assure her that she was right to confide in me. We were the same, after all!

I pushed my way back into the bar to the table where she was sitting, but she was no longer there. I looked around and bumped into Loz. I asked him if he had seen Jana anywhere and he said that she had already left, probably to go home. I had missed my chance. I sighed and then made my way back out to the smoking area to continue talking to the average one.

*

The average one's name was Amy. The gorgeous one's name was Celia. Guy had asked them if they wanted to continue the party back at our house and they had both agreed. We stopped off at an off-licence on the way back and bought some beer and real cigarettes. They had run out of liquid for their e-cigarettes and decided to just get the real things. Their lungs could afford to take one hit, they rationalised.

We got back to the house and went out to the back garden, where everyone smoked the cigarettes while drinking beer and talking. I wasn't engaging in much of the talking, smoking, or drinking, but I was trying to get involved where I could. I just let Guy take control, as he was good at making them laugh and keeping them interested. And, it wasn't long before Guy and Celia had begun kissing and fondling each other. Amy suggested that we go back inside, to which I agreed.

We sat at the kitchen table and the conversation wasn't nearly as smooth as when Guy was involved. It was also awkward because I wasn't sure whether I should make a move on her or not. I had never been in that situation before and didn't know what the etiquette was.

Guy and Celia rushed through the kitchen while giggling. On his way through Guy said, "Don't stay up too long, kids!" and ruffled my hair. He and Celia then ran upstairs and I heard the door to Guy's room slam shut.

I looked at Amy and she looked at me. She looked up at the ceiling and then tapped her beer can idly. Unsure of what to do, I went to the fridge and extracted another can. When I turned back around, Amy was standing there hovering over me and smiling. I closed my eyes and went in for the kiss, which to my relief was reciprocated. The more we kissed, the more impassioned she became; scraping her fingers through my hair, grabbing my arse and biting my lower lip. I tried to keep up, but I wasn't sure where my hands were supposed to be or what they should be doing. I also didn't know whether I should be playing it rough or tender, so I tried a little bit of both. I ran my hand gently up the nape of her neck, over her scalp and then grabbed a handful of her hair, tugging it back before lunging in with a passionate kiss. She seemed to like that and swung her head back towards me so that she could bite my ear in response. I pretended to enjoy that, but in actual fact, I was concentrating so much on whether I was doing things right that I didn't have time to consider whether it was enjoyable.

After the kissing had continued for some time, she grabbed my hand and asked me to lead her to my bedroom. It was hard to stop my hand shaking with nerves. I led her upstairs and into my room. We could hear Guy and Celia fucking each other in the room next door. She giggled and I giggled too, but the reality was that I was terrified. I knew there was no way I could match Guy's performance. She sat me down on the bed and slowly peeled off my borrowed T-shirt. The neck hole was a bit tight and a strong tug was required to get it over my head. She threw it on the floor. I tried to take off her clothes, but the whole thing was a struggle. Every item of clothing was stubborn and seemed to be tenaciously bound to her body in some way: tight T-shirt, extra tight jeans, complicated boots, impossible bra. I noticed the boredom etched on her face as she sat there watching me struggle with her clothing. She pushed me off and took it upon herself to remove the rest of the clothing. I didn't even get to see her naked, as she turned the light off before removing her underwear. It was almost pitch black, except for a few small gleams of light peering in through the cracks in the Venetian blind. She had also crawled under the blanket as quickly as she could. I removed the last of my clothing too and crawled under the blankets with her where we began kissing again. I moved my hand over her breast and squeezed it softly. It was the first time I had ever touched a breast before. She didn't seem too impressed with my foreplay and put her hand over mine and squeezed my hand to indicate that I needed to grab her breast harder. We did this for a while and I started to get bored. Not being able to see her face or see what I was touching increased the abstract nature of the activity. I couldn't connect the feeling to reality, or fully experience what I was doing. I felt my erection begin to soften as a result of this and decided that I just had to achieve penetration before it became flaccid and useless. I rolled over her and held myself up over her body. I reached down and got hold of my dick, but as I was not able to see a damned thing that I was doing, I just randomly poked it at her. I missed, and I think it hit her inner thigh. I tried another time, but again - nowhere near her vagina. I shoved my hand under the sheets and felt around. I came across a hot, wet, sticky opening which I guessed was her vagina and tried to guide my dick inside. But again, it didn't slide in. It just hit the pelvic bone and bounced back out. She sighed and I said that I was sorry. She put her hand under the covers, grabbed my dick and slowly guided it inside of her, groaning lightly as she did so. I was relieved that it was finally in, but what was I supposed to do next? Was I meant to penetrate slow or fast, tender or rough, slowly then faster, faster, then slowly, then faster again while being tender and rough at the same time? I chose to just move in and out of her at a medium pace in a mechanical fashion. I couldn't see her facial expression, but in my mind, I imagined it to be one of disinterest and disappointment. I tried pumping faster and then I tried doing it slower, but she barely exhibited any reaction regardless of which approach I took.

And, as I pumped away on her in that hollow, infinite darkness, I wondered why people made such a big fuss over having sex. Maybe it was just the room's darkness that led to it being such a strange and removed experience, maybe because it was my first time, or maybe it just really wasn't as good as people made it seem. Our bodies just seemed to fall away, and we became the abyss of the room. No light or understanding, just a concept of a feeling or a gap in the concept itself. An overwhelming feeling of the absurd hit me and I burst out laughing.

She pushed me off and her disembodied voice angrily demanded to know what was so funny. I told her that I didn't know why I was laughing. She rolled over, put her back to me and that was that. It didn't matter to me anyway, my dick had gone soft and there was no way of reviving it.

*

I awoke early the next day; it was around dawn I think. She was still sleeping next to me. The room was now exposed by the light from outside. I could see her face in the dim early morning glare. She was sleeping soundly. I wondered if I could just creep out of my own room and leave her there pretending that the whole thing had never happened. Or, I could creep out of my own skin and never return - a hollow body in a hollow world.

I didn't want to have to talk to her when she woke up and I'm sure she had no interest in talking to me either. I slipped on my underwear and T-shirt, as I felt exposed sleeping naked. I laid back down on the bed and listened to see if I could hear anything from Guy's room next door, but all was quiet. Everything was quiet.

I closed my eyes and looked to see what the insects thought of the situation, but the shelves were bare -

they had gone. They weren't watching over me anymore. I thought back to what Jana had said the previous night. This external pressure, this other thing that was watching over her. This "other". I became profoundly depressed. Her statement resonated with me and created a connection between the two of us. I had never felt that affected by someone else's words. So, why had I not reacted? Was it too much of a shock? Was I too keen to sleep with this average Amy beside me? Was I too average myself? I had now blown it with Jana, and I knew that. Could I try to apologise? Probably not. It was too late. I had missed my opportunity and she must have regretted ever opening up to me. The more I opened myself up to Guy's culture, the more I became lost. I was losing my sense of what connected me to reality. It was all too fast. I was just a fucking pervert in this world.

I closed my eyes and tried to forget everything. A wind picked up outside. It roared and howled as it battered the pane.

I awoke again later in the morning. Amy had begun to stir. I sat up and looked at her resurfacing into the waking world. She slowly opened her eyelids and for the briefest of moments, she appeared happy until she realised that she wasn't in her own bed. She groaned and sat up holding the blanket over her chest. I said good morning to her and she replied with a good morning back. Then, there was silence - the morning interaction was even more awkward than I had anticipated. She definitely wasn't the chatty, happy-go-lucky person that she had been the night before. She seemed miserable and ashamed. She asked where her friend Celia was, and I told her that I assumed that she was still in Guy's room. I hadn't heard from them since the previous night.

She asked me to pass her clothes to her and she proceeded to get dressed under the bedsheets. I also put on the rest of my clothes. We did this in silence. I couldn't wait for her to leave my room, and I think she thought the same. When she was dressed, she asked where Guy's room was, and I showed her. She knocked on his door and called out for Celia. After knocking twice, Celia responded. I could hear through the door that she was giggling and flirting with Guy. They were definitely not experiencing the same awkwardness that Amy and I were suffering. Celia told Amy just to wait for a while, but Amy insisted that she wanted to leave immediately. Celia finally conceded and told her that she would be ready in half hour.

I took Amy to the kitchen, where we waited for Guy and Celia to have one more fuck session. I made Amy a cup of tea and we sat at the kitchen table trying to look anywhere but at each other. She asked if I had worn a condom the previous night. I told her that I didn't have one, but I didn't come inside her so there shouldn't be a problem. She grimaced and told me that you don't have to come to spread an STI. I told her that there was absolutely no chance that I had an STI and not to worry about it. She turned her head away. The conversation was painful and was then made even worse when Jana came into the kitchen to get something from the fridge.

She looked at us both before hurriedly getting what she wanted out of the fridge and scurrying out of the room. Amy texted Celia for her to hurry up and come down - she got no reply.

Finally, after what felt like an eon, Guy and Celia emerged from the room and came downstairs. The whole time, they were laughing and couldn't keep their hands off each other. They came into the kitchen and Amy gave Celia a deathly stare. Celia knew she was in trouble. They left promptly. Guy and Celia made sure that they had exchanged numbers before they parted, but Amy and I suggested no such thing to each other.

When they were gone, Guy grabbed me and hugged me tightly. "I'm so fucking proud of you, buddy. You really stood up to the challenge last night. Now, you've got that monkey off your back, the world is your oyster! How do you feel? Great, I bet!"

I told him that I did indeed feel great and thanked him for fulfilling his promise.

"No problem," he said. "I've shown you the way, so it's all down to you, now. I mean, Celia was great and everything, but I can do better. I was only talking to those two so that you could get your end away."

We left the conversation at that. Guy went off to have a shower, and as none of the other housemates were around, I went back to my room to catch up on the box sets that I had been watching. I was determined to catch up and be able to talk freely about them.

*

By Monday evening, I had crammed in all the box sets and films that I could handle and had memorised all the plot lines and characters. I was fully prepared to converse about them with the other housemates. I had also listened to all the music that they had recommended and researched the band's histories online. I had also found an interesting recipe that had received numerous positive reviews and decided to suggest making it with everyone. I went to the kitchen and waited for the other housemates to return. There was no sign of any of them. I waited and waited, then decided to just start the recipe myself. It was a difficult recipe to execute and I had trouble with it from the outset. Without Guy's help, I realised that I just wasn't very good at cooking. When it was finished the meal didn't look anything like it was supposed to and also none of the housemates had returned home yet. I tested the meal and knew that it tasted like shit; even my indifferent taste buds could sense that. I scraped the whole lot into the bin and made myself scrambled egg on toast instead.

While I was eating, one of the housemates finally returned home. It was Loz. I waited for him in the kitchen but instead, he headed straight for his room and closed the door. I contemplated going to his room and knocking on his door, but I thought better of it. I waited longer, and after a while, Will and Oscar also came back home. They came into the kitchen and I could smell alcohol on their breath. I asked them where they had been, and they simply said that they had been out. I told them about the recipe that I had thought looked nice and they replied they had already eaten a curry that night. They got another couple of beers out of the fridge and had one each without bothering to offer me one. I thought I would impress them with my newly acquired knowledge of the programs I had been watching and began to recap what had happened in the final episode. I told them how riveting it was and praised its writing. Will simply concurred that it was a good episode and then they excused themselves to go out for a cigarette. I grabbed a beer for myself, sat down on the kitchen table and began drinking. It was getting late and there was still no sign of Guy. Loz appeared from his room and came into the kitchen. When he saw me, he simply asked where the others were. I told him they were outside smoking a cigarette. He said that he would join them and went out to the garden.

I sat down and continued to drink the beer, waiting for them to come back inside, but they didn't. I could hear them laughing and joking with each other in the garden, and after a while, I became tired of sitting on my own and decided to go out and join them.

They were not smoking cigarettes - they were smoking a long joint. I asked if I could join them and they agreed. Will passed me the joint and I took a drag. I suppressed the need to cough and splutter, attempting to blow out the smoke as casually as I could. I sensed that the conversation had quietened with my presence, so I decided to try and talk to them about some of the music I had been listening to, and also mentioned that I had watched a film that they had recommended. They nodded in approval, but didn't seem to be engaged in the conversation. I then turned to discussing our night out the previous Friday evening. I brought up some of the things that had happened, but they weren't very responsive. Their recollection of the night was different to mine. They had ended up at the DJ's afterparty and so they began to reminisce about that instead. They began to recall incidents from the afterparty, and I felt completely left out. When the joint was finished, we all went back inside, and I sat at the kitchen table expecting them to do the same, but instead, they told me that they were going to Loz's room to play a computer game with their friends online. They didn't suggest that I join them; instead, they just walked straight into Loz's room and left me sitting alone. I guessed that they did not ask me to join them as I had not shown any interest in gaming. There had been so many facets of culture to learn that some things, like gaming, had to take a back seat.

I continued to sit at the table and wait for Guy. There was nothing in my room to do now, and I could not force-feed myself any more box sets, films, or music for the time being. I could hear Loz, Will, and Oscar all shouting through their gaming headsets while enthusiastically playing the game. I thought about going into the room and asking to sit and watch them, but I didn't want to push things too far.

Guy came back later, almost as I was ready to go to bed. He was very drunk and came into the kitchen to grab a snack from the fridge. I asked him where he had been.

"What are you, my wife?" he replied, half-jokingly.

I laughed the comment off and said that I was curious, that's all.

"I'm only joshing you, Nil. Lighten up. Just been pounding the brews with some of the lads from work. Great lot. Celebrating another promotion for yours truly." He held out his arms triumphantly. "I am smashing it over at that firm!"

I congratulated him and raised my empty beer bottle to toast his success. Furthermore, as we were on that subject, I took the opportunity to ask him if he could find me any work at his place. I told him that I was willing to start at the bottom - anything would do. I said that I was finding it hard to get a job that I could enjoy and that I could really use some help.

"Sorry, Nil." he said, taking some chorizo sausage from the fridge. "It doesn't work that way. I don't do the hiring."

I asked him if he at least knew of any vacancies.

"I don't, mate. I don't look at that sort of stuff. Your best bet is to go to agencies or look on our website to see if there are any openings. I'm sure you'll be fine."

I said that I just hoped I could find something soon. I was rapidly running out of money.

"I'm sure you'll be fine," he reiterated as he was walking out of the room. "If not, just see if you can get your old job back. I'm sure they'll take you if you go back with your tail between your legs."

I told him that I wouldn't enjoy doing that job.

"Well, you can't afford that luxury at the moment, dude!"

And with that, he left the kitchen and went to Loz's room. He opened the door and screamed, "I got the promotion, bitches!" to which they all cheered and congratulated him. Then, he entered the room and joined in with their game.

I sat alone and toyed with my empty beer bottle. I again briefly contemplated going to Loz's room and joining in, but I knew that was a bad idea, so I just went to bed instead.

This kind of thing went on for a few days. The housemates never seemed to be around anymore. I spent my time waiting in the kitchen and hanging around, but they mostly preferred to stay in their rooms. When I did catch sight of one of them, I would try to strike up a conversation about music, films, TV or art, but they showed no interest in what I was saying. I didn't really understand what I was doing wrong, but the atmosphere in the house had changed. It seemed that they were trying to avoid something.

On Thursday, I awoke to the loud slamming of the front door. I came out of my room and saw that the door to Jana's room was ajar, which I thought was strange as it was usually closed. I approached her room and called out her name, but there was no response. I slowly pushed the door open and peeked inside. The room was empty apart from the bed and wardrobe. All her stuff had gone, only the faint aroma of her fragrance was left behind. I ran downstairs and out of the front door to see if I could catch her before she left, but she was already gone. I would never see her again.

I went back inside the house and into her room, where I just sat, inhaling her diminishing scent. I seemed to be doing everything wrong. I was sincerely trying to do all that was being asked of me, but it still wasn't working. I was trying to talk like them, act like them, watch the same things, listen to the same music, eat the same foods, engage in the same interests, have the same thoughts, and fuck like them, yet it didn't seem to be enough. I realised that even though I was doing the things that were being asked of me, I wasn't actually enjoying them. Was I not getting it? Was I doing something wrong? Or, was I simply not capable of feeling this sense of enjoyment that came so easily to the others?

I had to up my game. I had to actually experience the enjoyment of these things instead of simply pretending. I returned to my room and spent the day trying to actually feel the music instead of just listening to it. I tried to engage emotionally in a film instead of simply studying it. And, I tried to masturbate to porn instead of using it as a guide on how to have sex. Nevertheless, the feeling still didn't come. I knew that if I wanted to understand the others, I'd have to get out there and experience it for myself first-hand. It wasn't good enough to be cooped up in my room and trying to experience everything from a distance. I messaged Guy and asked him if he was up for going out that night, but he replied saying that he needed to be up early for work the next day. I needed to create my own narrative. I decided that I would go out that evening and see where the evening took me. I would immerse myself in the experience, rather than watching from the sidelines or waiting for Guy to do it for me.

I still hadn't returned the clothes that I had borrowed the other night. I straightened out the T-shirt that was still in a crumpled heap on the floor and put it on, but I couldn't find the jeans. After some searching around, I found them under the bed, and as I pulled them out, they brought with them one of my insects - a *Blaberus craniifer* . It must have slipped under the bed when I was packing them up for the buyer. I took the insect that was stored pristinely in its glass case, held it up and gazed at the empty "eyes" in the strange markings on the back of it's head . A spontaneous wave of anger washed over me and I threw the case to the floor, causing it to smash on impact. The insect, now freed from its case, scuttled away and escaped from the room. I stood there in shock. Knowing that it must have been some sort of hallucination, I got on my knees and searched around for the escaped insect, but it was nowhere to be found. All that was left was the remains of the shattered case. It was gone.

I pulled on my jeans and shoes and picked up my wallet. I wasn't going to let a weird incident like that ruin my night, so I chose to erase it from my mind and I left the house. The insects weren't going to drag me back to my old life; I knew where that had gotten me. I was determined to see this new life through.

*

I went back to the same area where Guy had taken us only a few days ago. I started by going for food somewhere first. It was a trendy place that sold pizzas with pretentious names. It was all kitted out in chrome counters and wooden flooring, and the price of one slice was the same as a whole pizza elsewhere. Still, it was packed, and people were readily buying the overpriced slices and chomping them down. I bought a slice of the meatiest one and took it over to a table where I sat down. I watched the other diners as they ate, and I wondered what their plans were for the night ahead. I had no idea where I was going to go yet, and I needed some suggestions.

There was a group sitting on the table next to me and without procrastinating, I leant over and asked if they knew of any decent bars in the area. They all stopped talking and looked at me like I had just slapped one of them around the face with my pizza slice. One patronisingly said that there were loads of great places in the area, all I had to do was stick my head out of the door and I would see one. I thanked him for his help.

I sat back and studied him out of the corner of my eye. He slid his pizza slice into his mouth and ripped off a piece. The cheese stretched and when it finally snapped, it swung back onto his face. He slurped the dangling string of cheese up into his mouth, leaving a slither of grease behind that glistened on his bearded chin. He then told a banal anecdote to his friends about one of his escapades while constantly laughing at his own jokes. I wondered how such an unbelievable cunt could have so many friends. But, when I looked at his friends, it made sense - they were all cunts too.

I finished off my slice and walked out of there. I tried my hardest to work out how they could justify the extra money for that pizza. Was I paying for the decor, the silly names of the pizzas, the atmosphere, the clientele? I guessed it was for the whole experience in general and recognised that I should just stop thinking so much about all that kind of stuff. I just had to feel and not think. I suppose the retro neon signs they had in there were a nice touch.

I did what the arsehole at the table next to me had suggested and stuck my head out of the door to look around. He was right, there was a lot going on in the area. People were beginning their nights out, all with the optimism of what stories possibly lay ahead of them. I wondered what stories were in store for me. I couldn't see anything in my future at that moment, though. It was all up for grabs.

A young woman standing outside a bar called me over and told me that I could have a free shot of tequila if I went in and bought a drink. So, that's what I did. However, apart from the bartender and a couple drinking quietly in the corner, it was empty. I asked the bartender for a pint of beer, and she replied that they only sold bottles. I ordered a bottle of beer, and when she gave it to me, I reminded her of the free shot of tequila. She rolled her eyes and poured me my shot. She gave me a dirty slice of lemon and pointed to an even dirtier salt shaker. I didn't know what to do with the lemon or the salt shaker, so I just downed the tequila straight. It tasted like acid. I struggled to keep it down and ended up burping loudly. The bartender rolled her eyes again, so I took the beer and found a table.

It was very dark inside. I assumed that it had to be dark to cover the fact that it was a dingy shithole. And yet, the dimmed light couldn't mask the smell, which was that of sodden wood and sewage pipes. I quickly realised why it was so empty and why they needed a young, good-looking woman at the door to coax people in.

I drank my beer and watched the couple in the corner. They were more concerned with what was on their phones than with each other. Were they bored with each other, or was this how people interacted?

I quickly finished the rest of my bottle of beer and got out of there. I needed more action than that place could provide.

I escaped to the main street again and began to search around. I saw that there was a bar with loud music pumping through the walls and people milling around inside. I decided to try it out.

I got into the queue and waited about ten minutes to get in. It was still early evening, so I was surprised that it was already so popular. At the door, I was frisked by a doorman. He asked me if I was meeting anyone inside and I told him that I was on my own. He screwed up his face and looked me up and down. I explained to him that I was meant to be meeting someone later, I was just early, that was all. He unscrewed his face and waved me in.

The inside was crowded, and everyone was carrying drinks and barging to get from one spot to another. I fought my way to the bar and waited a good twenty minutes to get served. I had to scream at one of the bartenders so that he recognised my presence.

When I was finally in possession of my beer, I tried to find a spot where I could stand and drink calmly, but it was impossible. Wherever I stood, there was someone ready to stab me in the back with their elbow as they vied to get past, which caused them to either spill their drink over me or me to spill my own drink on myself.

There were groups of young pretty women everywhere. I couldn't fathom how I would manage to talk to any of them, but I knew that I had to try. I noticed a pair standing on the other side of the room chatting to each other. I decided to approach them, as talking to two girls was less daunting than trying to infiltrate a larger group. I barged my way through the crowd, using my elbows like the others had done to me, and managed to get near them. I watched them as they spoke to each other, and I wondered how I could insert myself into their conversation. I thought of what Guy would do and then did the same.

I leaned in and asked them if they were enjoying their night so far. They looked at me and screwed up their faces, much like the doorman had done earlier. I instantly realised that this was a lame question. They told me that they were just happy chatting amongst themselves. I wouldn't be defeated that easily, so I told them that I was new to the area and was just looking to find like-minded people who could show me some good places. They told me that I had interrupted their conversation and reiterated that they were happy just talking to each other. I backed off and left them alone. I obviously didn't have Guy's looks, charm or confidence. Or, maybe I had just picked the wrong targets.

I spotted a girl sitting on her own on one of the sofas positioned around the perimeter of the room. I waited for a while to see if she was waiting for a friend or a boyfriend to return. Ten minutes passed and still no-one showed, so I concluded that she was there alone. I psyched myself up, went over to the sofa and sat down next to her. But, as soon as my buttocks touched the fabric of the sofa cushion, she indicated firmly that she was waiting for her boyfriend. I didn't even manage to say a word. I extracted myself from the sofa and slunk away.

I ordered more beer at the bar, followed by more beer, and then even more beer. All the while, the place continued to fill up with more people, with increasingly more heat, more sweat, more elbows, and more frustration. I couldn't bear it any longer so I pushed my way through the densely packed human flesh and made my way to the street outside. I was relieved to be out of the bar. The doorman remarked that there was no re-entry and I told him that I was fine with that.

I walked around for a bit before finding a pub with a more traditional decor. This one wasn't as packed as the bar and had a more relaxed atmosphere. Even so, all the tables were occupied, so I stood at the bar and had my drink. I was the only one standing and drinking, so I felt awkward. A young woman approached the bar to buy a drink and I offered to buy the drink for her, which she accepted. She was friendlier than the others had been, but as soon as her drink arrived, she walked off and ended the conversation while I was still mid-sentence. What was I doing wrong?

I finished my drink and went back out to the street. People around me were starting to get drunk, and I was joining them. A cab driver, seeing that I was confused, asked me if I needed a ride anywhere. I got in his cab and told him to take me to a place where there were women. A lot of women. He gave me the thumbs-up and off we went.

*

The cab driver let me out at a strip club, and before I had time to think about it, I was handing over my money for the entrance charge. This time, the doorman didn't care if I was alone or not. He didn't even look at me as he waved me in.

I walked through the doors and into the main area. The place did not have the appearance of what I thought was a stereotypical strip club. It seem liked a regular bar, except there were women walking around in skimpy lingerie and bikinis. The club was full of men, most of whom were in groups, but there were also some, like me, who were alone. The loners just stood around the sides and watched the action from afar or planted themselves at the front of the stage to get the best possible view. There were also women, and I don't mean strippers. I mean normal women on a night out. They were mostly mingled in with some of the groups of men. They had probably been convinced by the men or convinced themselves that it would be a wacky experience. However, now that they were there, they seemed to be uncomfortable, but pretended to enjoy the situation at the same time. For the lone men, it wasn't a one-off wacky experience at all - it was a lifestyle.

Before I could even get to the bar, I felt a hefty bosom press up against my side and a pair of wet glossy lips kiss my cheek. I turned around to see a sinewy woman in high heels, a thong and a bra standing before me. She asked me what my name was, where I was from, if I was enjoying my night, and if I wanted to see her pussy. I stumbled over my words and politely declined. She could tell that I was an inexperienced dupe and persisted, trying to get me to go for a private dance. I calmed my nerves and firmly yet still politely told her that I wasn't ready. She conceded and walked off.

I got a drink and stood by the bar watching the action. It seemed safer at the bar for some reason. I watched as an older man and a stripper sat on a sofa in a cornered-off area where they flirted and drank champagne. She didn't look like she was even trying to pretend that she was enjoying it. I wondered how much the man must be paying for that experience.

It wasn't long before another stripper approached me. This one was small and rounder than the previous one. Again, she asked me what my name was, where I was from, if I was enjoying my night, and if I wanted to see her pussy. I told her that I had just arrived and maybe we could go for a dance later.

I was in awe of the amount of flesh on show and wasn't really sure where to look. I had never experienced anything like it before.

The music stopped and the DJ introduced the next stripper who would be dancing on stage. Some of the men took that as their cue to flock to the stage so they could get as close to the action as possible. The DJ told everyone to give her a round of applause, although only a few people actually clapped.

A new song started, and she took to the stage. She began her dance by gyrating her hips and then suddenly, she flung her body onto the pole, turned herself upside down and split her legs wide apart. Her countenance, all the while, was one of grim despair. She proceeded to remove her clothes until she was completely naked. She continued her frantic dance of gloom until the song had finished, whereupon she retrieved her clothes and walked off stage. The DJ asked everyone to clap for the show, but again only a few did, and it was a half-hearted clap at that.

Another stripper approached me. She was huge. Not fat, but huge. I felt like a small boy in her shadow. She asked me what my name was, where I was from, if I was enjoying my night, and if I wanted to see her pussy. I was beginning to sense a pattern emerging. As with the previous strippers, I declined her offer. I was intrigued though, and wanted to know what a private dance would be like. I looked around the room to see if there were any women that piqued my interest. There were some nice ones, but none that were outstanding. Suddenly I saw one. She was amazing. In fact, she reminded me of Jana. She had thick black hair and a face that was vaguely similar, but it was her unassuming demeanour that was identical. I couldn't take my eyes off her. Unlike the other strippers, she wasn't doing the rounds and pestering men for dances. Instead, she was standing in the corner looking bored and fed up. I wondered if I should ask her for a dance when she was obviously so indifferent to the whole thing. I continued to watch her, and after I had finished my drink, I made up my mind to go over and talk to her. On my way over, another stripper stopped me and asked me what my name was, then where I was from. I put up my hand to stop her before she could continue and told her that I didn't want a dance. She looked angry that she wasn't allowed to complete the necessary spiel and stormed off.

When I got to the Jana look-a-like, I stood and glared at her. She didn't take any notice of me, though. I tapped her on the shoulder and she slowly turned towards me.

She feigned a weak smile. I asked her what her name was, where she was from, if she was enjoying her night, and then I asked to see her pussy. She told me it was twenty pounds for a dance and I agreed.

She led me back to the dimly lit private dance area. She sat me down in an empty booth, took a twenty-pound note from me and proceeded to dance. But, it wasn't so much of a dance, more of a disinterested swaying of the body. She took off her top and then her bottoms. She laid on the floor, spread her legs and then spread her pussy. I stared up and into her body. I didn't know whether to be aroused or disgusted; maybe I felt a combination of the two. She turned over, got on all fours with her back to me and then pulled her buttocks apart so I could see deep into her arsehole. Then, she got back up and pushed her breasts together in front of my face. I reached out and touched her body, but she instantly pushed my arms away and scolded me. Apparently, there was no contact allowed. At the end of the dance, she asked me if I wanted another one and I told her that one was enough. It was more like a medical examination than something seductive or sexy.

I went back out into the main area and bought a shot. I downed it, then ordered another one. I leant back onto the bar to keep my balance - I was drunk. My head was spinning, and I felt sick. I rushed to a cubicle in the toilet and puked in the bowl. I overheard some men who were having a piss in the urinals. They were raving about what a great time they were having and that they couldn't believe how brilliant the private dances were. Was I in the same place as them? What was I missing? What was this essential quality that everyone was experiencing that I just couldn't grasp?

I flushed the toilet, but it was clogged and began to overflow. Vomit and shit started to rise from the depths and threatened to spill over the edge of the bowl. The smell was putrefying. Insects began to gather. They were crawling over the floors, up the cubicle walls and over the ceiling.

I battled my way out of the toilet and back into the main bar. There were insects everywhere. They were all giant insects: the strippers, the men, the bartenders, all of them. Huge disgusting insects twitching and writhing over each other. A tangled mess of antennae, mandibles and huge black empty eyes. Foraging, feeding, and fornicating. Their little minds were the product of unthinking mechanics and instinct. A rank smell filled the air. I looked down and saw that I was standing in black sludge. The toilets had overflown completely, and raw sewage was filling the room. I recoiled and held my hand over my nose and mouth to block out the smell. The insects loved it, though. They rolled in the sludge and covered their bodies in the mess. All of them together in an orgy of the depraved.

I turned for the door, running back into the street in an effort to get some fresh air. I calmed down and tried to clear my mind. I puffed and panted like I had run a thousand miles.

A cab driver asked me if I needed a lift. I said that I did, and he led me to his car. He was already driving before I had a chance to tell where I wanted to go. I sat back on the seat, calmed myself down and realised that the whole thing was just my intoxicated mind playing tricks on me. I looked out of the window and saw that the world was normal again. No giant insects and no black sludge. Just the regular shitty world. The cab driver asked me if I liked strippers. I didn't answer. He said that strippers were good, but not as good as the real thing. I said that I didn't know what he meant. He replied that the problem with strippers was that you couldn't touch. I agreed with him. He then casually suggested that he could take me to a place where I could touch. A place with very nice girls; he assured me that I would enjoy myself very much. I shrugged and told him that I needed to enjoy something. He smiled widely and promised me that I would not be disappointed.

After a short drive, the cab driver pulled up in front of a row of shops. He pointed to a flat above one of the shops and told me to press the buzzer and ask for someone called Jaz. I got out of the cab and did what he said. I was buzzed up.

I walked up some dank, creaky stairs and came to a small landing. There were two doors - one on either side of the landing. I looked at each one. Which one to choose? I knocked on the door to the left and the door edged open. A woman stood there in a dressing gown and invited me to enter. I went in and she told me to sit on the bed. Although the room was dark and bathed in a gloomy red light emitted by a bedside lamp, I could still tell that she was in her mid-thirties. Her face was haggard and sad, and it looked like she was on the brink of suicide. She said that it would be fifty pounds for twenty minutes. I didn't reply, which she took as a sign to proceed. She took off her gown and stood naked over me. Her breath stank and so did her vagina. She pulled my T-shirt over my head and then unzipped my fly. She pulled out my flaccid dick and rubbed it. Nothing. She rubbed it harder and then put her stinking mouth around it and began to suck it mechanically. Nothing. She sucked harder. Still nothing. She pulled her head away and I tucked my soft dick back into my trousers. She told me that I'd still have to pay regardless.

As she was getting dressed, I asked her if there was something wrong with me. She told me it was normal, particularly when someone was drunk as I was. I said that I didn't mean that, I meant was there something wrong with me that I didn't know how to enjoy? How can I get this feeling, how can I learn how to enjoy experiences?

She stopped getting dressed and looked at me. She smiled grimly, her crooked teeth shining like blood under the red light. She looked like she was on the cusp of imparting some deep wisdom. She put her hand on my shoulder and sweetly said that there was no fucking way I was going to get out of paying her. I got out my wallet, gave her the money and left.

The cab driver had gone when I got back out onto the street and I had no idea where I was. The roads were quiet and there were no other cars in sight. I was too drunk to work out how to download and sign up for a cab app, or even to walk around and find a main street. I noticed a small park on the other side of the road. I entered the park and collapsed under a large tree. I laid in the dirt and began to blubber uncontrollably. Tears poured from my eyes faster than I could wipe them away. I pressed my face into the mud and cried into the ground until I passed out.

*

The next day, I trudged back to the house, throwing up intermittently along the way. When I arrived, it was still early morning, so I took a shower then went to bed. I woke up again in the afternoon to sounds coming from out in the hall. I looked outside my door and saw that there was a new tenant moving in to Jana's old room. He was making one hell of a racket moving his stuff around. I approached him and introduced myself. He told me that his name was Sean and that he had just moved over from Ireland. I said to him that he had made a good choice picking this house, as everyone was friendly and that we had a great time together. This seemed to please him and we made small talk for a while. Afterwards, I asked him if he needed a hand bringing his stuff in and he said that extra hands would be appreciated. I figured that because he had only just arrived from Ireland, he would barely have anything with him, so it would be an easy favour. However, it turned out that he had brought his car over on the ferry and he had a whole estate that was filled to the brim with his shit. After we had unloaded the stuff from the car and unpacked it in his room, he asked if I wanted to take a trip to a furniture outlet store to buy some cupboards and shelves. I agreed, so we got in his car and he began to drive. On the way, I bombarded him with my newly acquired knowledge of film, TV, music, clubbing, food, travel and lifestyle. It was like I had a checklist and just reeled off one reference point after another. Sean could hardly keep up as I rambled on and on. I was also trying to be as positive about everything as I could. I told him again how great the housemates were and how much fun the house was. I told him about the bars and clubs that I had been to and what an amazing scene there was in London. Sean just wore a daft grin and nodded as I prattled on and on.

He quickly chose the furniture that he wanted, and we brought it back to the house. I asked if he wanted my help with assembling everything, but he told me that I had done enough for him already. With nothing else to do, I went down to the kitchen, grabbed a beer from the fridge, sat at the table and waited for the others.

Loz came back home and went straight into his room. I suddenly realised that all the doors to the other housemates' rooms were closed, which was not usually the case. Even when they weren't in, the doors were usually left ajar. I wondered if they were all in their rooms trying to avoid something; maybe it was me they were trying to avoid. I waited in the kitchen to assess the situation, and sure enough, after a few minutes, Oscar came out of his room and went straight into Loz's room and closed the door. I then heard footsteps from the room above, which mean meant that Will was also home.

What was going on? Why were they avoiding me? What had I done?

I continued to drink my beer, my anger growing with every swig. I had done everything that they asked. I had integrated myself into the houseshare, watched all the same programs, listened to all the same music, been to all the same places, made myself into a carbon copy of their lives, humiliated and debased myself to fit in, and now they were hiding from *me*?

I finished my beer, marched over to Loz's room and knocked on the door. Loz answered it and casually greeted me; I could see Oscar sitting on the floor playing a computer game on the TV. I adopted a pleasant tone and informed them that a new housemate had arrived and that the polite thing to do was to welcome him into the house. They looked at each other and said of course they would. I told them to wait in the kitchen. I then went upstairs and got Will out of his room too. I knocked on Guy's door, but he wasn't home yet. We all convened in the kitchen where I introduced Sean to the rest of the housemates. Polite conversation ensued and while we were talking, Guy finally arrived home. He saw us all in the kitchen and for the first time, he actually looked exasperated by the situation. He came into the kitchen to see what was going on. He introduced himself to the new housemate and I eagerly suggested that we all go to the pub to welcome Sean to the house. Neither Loz, Will, nor Oscar looked too enthused by that idea, and Guy mentioned that his promotion meant that he was working harder and was feeling exhausted. I informed them that it was a tradition we followed for all new housemates, and Guy conceded.

"You're right, Nil," Guy said, "It's only decent that we welcome the new arrival with a visit to the pub, but nothing heavy, as I have to be up early tomorrow."

Sean looked perplexed, but he agreed to the invite. He said that he looked forward to getting to know everyone in more depth. Guy went upstairs to drop his bag off in his room and then we all left for the pub.

In the pub, I told Sean that it was our tradition for the new housemate to buy the first round of drinks; I turned back and gave a cheeky wink to the others, to which there was no reaction.

We took the drinks over to a spare table and I toasted Sean's arrival. Sean instantly fit in with the others. He didn't necessarily watch the same things or listen to the same music, but he seemed to speak the same language as they did, and he was a fan of gaming and football. They all talked at length about which genre of computer game was the best. Will said RPGs, Loz and Oscar loved the third-person shooters, Guy couldn't make his mind up, and Sean said that if he had to choose, then it would be football simulations to coincide with his passion for real football. Then, there was a huge discussion about football and which teams they supported and about all the different competitions, leagues, and players. I was completely left out of the conversation. I hadn't had time to learn about any of those things. After being omitted from the conversation for a while, I interjected by bringing up a TV program that I knew they all liked watching. I recalled one of the episodes.

"Yeah, we know you like that one, Nil. You've told us before... A lot of times, actually," Guy quipped.

This instigated raucous laughter among the others. Even Sean laughed as apparently I had mentioned that program and also that particular episode while in the car on the way to the furniture store. I felt embarrassed, and I began to realise why they had been avoiding me. I looked down into my pint, not wanting to meet their judgmental eyes.

"Oh, don't be like that, Nil. I was only taking the piss. I'm glad we got you into those things, but you need to develop your interests a bit. Enjoy other things, too," Guy said patronisingly.

I looked up and smiled weakly, saying that I was man enough to take a joke and asked if they wanted another pint of beer. They all said yes, except Guy who told me to make his a shandy.

I went to the bar and ordered five lagers and a shandy. Then, in addition to the beers, I ordered ten shots of vodka. The bartender loaded them all up on a tray and I took them over to the table. They all looked shocked when I placed the tray down in front of them. I told them it was my treat to them for being such great housemates. Guy said that someone else could have his two shots as he had work the next day. Loz told me he had stuff to do and he didn't want to get wasted either. Will and Oscar also pushed theirs away. I looked at Sean who was petrified at the number of shots laid out before him. Nervously, he said that he didn't want any either, as he still had work to do on his room and spirits gave him a terrible hangover.

I sneered and commented that none of them knew how to enjoy themselves. I told them that they pretended to enjoy themselves but, in fact, they were all just fucking pussies. Who were they to tell me how to enjoy, when they didn't even know what the word meant? Well, if you know what it means then tell me what it means, you cunts, because I don't know how. Show me how! Is this how you enjoy? Is this how you fucking do it?

I snatched a shot off of the table and downed it. Then another. And another. The burning sensation in my throat didn't stop me. Another. Another. Vomit rising in my mouth didn't stop me. Another shot. Another shot. Gagging didn't stop me. Another shot. One more. Last one. All ten shots gone. I topped off the shots by downing my beer. That's how you enjoy! I shouted at them.

They all froze and stared at me, worried about what I might do next. I looked back at them, breathing heavily and staring at them with wide piercing eyes. I grimly smiled and proceeded to down another beer from the tray. After that was finished, I attempted to grab another beer but my coordination was fucked; I clumsily pawed at the glasses and knocked the rest of them over. The remaining three pints spilt all over the table and began pouring over everyone's legs. Guy was annoyed - he stood up and grabbed me by the shirt.

"Nil, you're going to puke. Go to the toilet and fucking sort yourself out," he said. I tried to wriggle free of his grip, but he was too strong. He shoved me towards the toilet, which caused me to stumble through the pub and fall into a group of men, knocking some of their drinks over in the process. One of the men turned to me and told me to go and buy them another round of drinks before he got really angry. I told him to fuck himself in the arse with his friend's dick. He told me that he would punch my lights out. I told him to go ahead. I told him that I wanted to feel his punch. I told him that I might enjoy a fight. Go on hit me, I would enjoy that. I would enjoy that a lot.

He looked at me. I was barely able to stand up. I was barely able to keep my eyes open. He said that I was pushing my luck, but he could see that I was drunk, so he'd let me off this time. But, he said what I did need to do was go and get him and his friends a round of drinks otherwise he wouldn't be able to control his actions. I calmed myself and told him I'd get them their drinks and apologised profusely to all of them.

I turned away and headed towards the bar. Suddenly, entering my vision, I saw the *Blaberus craniifer* that had escaped from the glass case the previous day. It was scuttling about on top of a nearby table. When it saw me, it stopped moving and looked at me. I was not at all surprised by its presence. I could sense it was trying to communicate something to me. It's feelers frantically probed the exterior of an empty beer glass. I knew what it wanted me to do.

I picked up the empty glass, turned back around and headed to the man. I screamed in demented anger and smashed him over the head with the glass. Blood poured from his skull and he screamed out in pain. That's when I finally felt it. I felt the feeling that I had been searching for. I felt the enjoyment. I enjoyed that. Smashing that prick over the head was the most enjoyable thing I had ever done.

I was so relieved at experiencing this feeling that I simply laughed at the sight of his friends bearing down on me. I laughed harder as they began punching and kicking me unabated. I laughed some more as I fell to the floor and felt only the intense pain of fists and boots ripping skin, breaking bones and bruising organs.

I stopped laughing when everything disappeared and all I could see was the escaped *Blaberus craniifer* in front of me. The kicks and punches, the bruises and blood, the sadness and humiliation all dissolved into the eyes on it's death's head. The insect had finally shown me what it meant to be alive. And then, I felt nothing at all.

THE INSECT

I opened my eyes. The world before me was a mess. My vision was blurred and confused. I didn't know where I was or who I was. I laid there disorientated and immobilised. I was a husk with no memory except for that of darkness, and the desperation to remember only led further into the darkness. I felt too weak to move. I felt too weak to breathe. I ran a hand over my body to make sure that I was there, that I existed below my head. It was an emaciated frame and it was painful to touch, but I confirmed that my body was still there. I was just numb. I needed to thaw.
I lay waiting for answers in my useless body and soon enough, flashes of the events that had led to my current predicament pierced my brain like a bad dream. I now felt sorry that I had remembered anything at all and realised what bliss it was being just a husk. I pressed my knuckles into my eye sockets and gave them a stern and

revitalising rub. I stared up at the ceiling and watched the world as it organised itself and came back into focus. I could see again.

But, there was nothing to see except for a white ceiling floating above me. I turned my head to the side and saw that I was in a hospital bed in a standard issue National Health Service room. It had basic furniture, the odour of sterilisation, white walls and white floors. White conformity. White eternity. There was a deliberate sense of emptiness to the room. It had to be like that; a room that had witnessed so many lives and deaths had to be neutral. A blank slate that absorbed stories then spat them out remembering nothing.

My mouth was dry. I needed water. I searched around my bed and found a call button. I pressed it and moments later a nurse arrived to check on me. She was happy to see that I had awoken and gave me a glass of water.

I asked her how long I had been out for and she said two days. I asked her if any serious damage had been done to my body. She changed my drip bag and told me that the doctor would be in shortly to go through everything with me. She left and I waited for the doctor. And waited. And waited.

I had nothing to do while I waited for the doctor to come, so I couldn't help but reflect on the events that had transpired in the pub. I remembered how drunk and irrational I had been. I never thought I could act that way. Did I really enjoy that moment where I had smashed a glass over that man's head, and what did that say about me? I realised that I had become so desperate in my quest for enjoyment that it led me to commit an act of lunacy. I was done with alcohol and I was done with trying to fit in with the housemates. Fuck them.

Finally, the doctor came in and apologised for taking such a long time to see me. He said that he was the only doctor working the shift and it was chaos in the hospital. He picked up my chart and briefly studied the details. He told me that I was extremely lucky to have escaped that beating without sustaining any long-term injuries, but I would be in pain while everything healed; my kidney had suffered trauma, so I might be pissing blood for a while too. He told me that I had received a total of forty stitches and those thugs had really done a number on me. He said that I would probably be in the hospital for another few days as long as there weren't any complications, which he couldn't foresee happening.

I thanked him. Before he left, he mentioned that the police wanted to get my version of what had happened that night, and they would come to speak to me when I was ready. I was going to ask him what had happened to the man whose head I had struck with the glass, but decided that I didn't care.

The doctor left and soon after, two nurses came in and told me that now that I had awoken, they were going to move me to the shared ward. I told them that I didn't want to share. I had had enough of sharing. They told me that I didn't have a choice and began wheeling my bed through the corridors. Fuck me, I thought, would I ever be able to get away from shared accommodation?

*

They left me in the shared ward, which resembled a mental asylum rather than a hospital room.

An old woman was lying in the bed next to me. She was deteriorating; her skin was weathered to the point that it had given up clinging to her skeleton and now just hung loosely off her body. Her hair had thinned and was as white as the hospital walls, each wiry strand springing off her scalp in a different direction. Her nails were yellowed and had been gnawed away by years of compulsive biting. Her teeth were no more: just red, raw gums that chewed the air as she breathed. Her whole body was decaying; death in waiting, a decrepit wreck that had nothing left to live for. Except for her eyes. Her eyes were still young. Huge piercing pale blue eyes that defied age and persisted despite the death and decay. She stared at me and I stared back, lost in the depths of those eyes. She opened her mouth slightly and it seemed like she was on the cusp of imparting some learned wisdom, but the words would just not come out of her toothless mouth. Her eyes then began to water. Was she crying? Did I look as bad to her as she looked to me? Were we the same? Did she see decay, death and hopelessness in my face too?

I leaned over and whispered to her, asking her what she saw when she looked at me. She glared coldly at me for a second and then she opened her mouth wide - so wide that it seemed that her jaw was bound by elastic. Then, she let out one huge deafening scream. Everyone in the ward covered their ears, except for me. It was a scream of pure naked horror that struck me to the core. A nurse came running in and shoved her hand over the old woman's mouth to try and cover the sound as if she was exposing some dark humiliating secret. I just closed my eyes and listened to the scream. To me, it was the voice of truth. The only thing that ever needed to be said. The hairs on my back stood on end. And, for once, I felt as though I understood what others might feel when they listened to music. This was my music.

Another nurse ran in with a needle and injected something into one of the large pulsating veins in the old woman's arm. She responded quickly to the drug and fell into a catatonic stupor. The nurses carefully laid her back down and drew the curtain around her bed. I heard no more from the old woman that night.

I spent my time in that ward watching the other patients being visited by their family and friends. No-one wanted to be there. The visitors spent the time looking at their phones or staring into thin air. When they did talk, it was always the same conversation, the same banal chitchat: You're looking better. Have you eaten? What is the food like? How are the nurses treating you? Who else has come to visit you today? You'll be out of here soon enough. Try to stay positive!

I was glad that I knew no-one would bother to come and visit me. So, that's why it came as a shock to see Guy bounding around the corner just before visiting hours were over. He wore a huge smile on his face and he looked at me like I was a lost puppy. He pulled up a chair and sat next to my bed. I was in the middle of my hospital dinner of dry chicken and mashed potatoes. Guy looked at the meal with a grimace.

"What's the food like?" he said.

I told him that it was fine.

"How are the nurses treating you in here?"

I told him that they were fine.

He fidgeted and looked around at the other patients in the ward. He watched as a large ugly man walked past wheeling his medical equipment beside him. The man's gown was loose and exposed his varicose-veined legs and occasionally his scrotum. It was a disgusting sight and Guy looked at the man like he was from another planet. People like that were the antithesis of Guy's world vision. Guy turned back to me and shook his head in revulsion at what he had just seen.

"Christ. I hate visiting hospitals," he said. "They give me the creeps."

I told him that it was no fun staying in one either.

"The others are sorry that they couldn't come to visit you, but they told me to send you their regards," he said blankly. We both knew that it wasn't true. "What those thugs did to you in the pub was out of order. We witnessed the whole thing. It was horrible. We thought they had killed you."

I said that they had nearly succeeded. Then, there was a silence. I rested my head back on the pillow and stared up at the white floating ceiling. I stared into the whiteness and asked Guy why they hadn't done anything to help me.

"You're blaming us?" Guy asked angrily. It was the first time I had ever heard him use an outright negative tone. Usually, when he had something negative or criticising to say, he would mask it as a joke or compliment. But, not this time. He had no reason to mask his true feelings now. "You were the one who was out of control, Nil," he continued. "What were we meant to do, jump in like it was the wild west and start a bar brawl? It was your fault that you were so drunk and it was you who started the fight. You smashed a fucking glass over the man's head, you psycho."

I casually told Guy that the man deserved it while continuing to stare aimlessly into the drifting white ceiling.

"He might have deserved it, but we didn't deserve to get dragged into it. We do not deserve you. You have been a problem since day one. I tried. I tried to help you out, but, but… but you're just fucking weird. At first, you wouldn't even talk to me. You wouldn't even look at me. I was beneath you. I was like a piece of shit to you, and you made every effort to shut me out even though I reached out to you. And then, you tell the landlord that I set fire to the kitchen and try and get me thrown out. But, I knew it was you who started that fire, you creep. You fucking… And then, you go missing for a week, probably crying about how I fucked Jana. Yeah, I fucked her good. That stupid bitch. She is just like you, another fucking creep. You would have been great together. She was a shit fuck anyway. It would have been perfect, you and her shit fucking forever more. But, you didn't fuck her, did you? I fucked her. I fucked her up the arse. Did you like it when I came on her arse? You pervert. You pervert with your creepy pathetic insects. You're the insect. It is you who is an insect."

I continued to stare at the floating white ceiling as he continued with his rambling tirade. I was floating with the ceiling - inside the white, lost in the white, becoming the white.

Guy leaned in even closer and continued. His voice lowered in volume but increased in vitriol. "And then, you come back after a week of going missing and you come to me and ask for help. The bare-faced cheek of it! Making a gumbo. The gumbo recipe that I was saving for a special occasion. The gumbo recipe that I was looking forward to sharing with my real friends. But, there you were, making my special recipe and asking me to save you. Asking me to help you enjoy your life. You snivelling piece of shit. At least have enough respect for yourself to stick to your guns. Don't come back crawling on your hands and knees, sucking up to me and asking to show you how to enjoy things. Are you for real? You don't even know how to enjoy your own life? Did you honestly think that you could go on a couple of nights out, watch a few box sets and listen to a few music tracks, then all of a sudden you would understand the meaning of existence? I've spent my life working at it, becoming part of it, learning how to connect with people and make friendships. Enjoyment isn't just a thing you do; it's a thing that you are. You can't just walk into it, you cretin. You know, I must admit that I envied you at the beginning, managing to live your life free of any these... these fucking constraints. These external pressures that tell us that we must be either this way or that way. You were outside of it all. How is that fair? Why do you get to live your life and not have to be a constant purveyor of positivity and conformity? How fucking dare you? What makes you so special that you're free of it? Do you think I like being the fucking perpetual centre of positivity and enjoyment? Sometimes I get angry, depressed, whatever. But, I put a positive face on it and I still make the effort to be civil to people and not inflict my problems on them, and it's hard, hard work sometimes. Then, you come along not giving a single shit. So, yes, I envied you at the beginning. I will admit that. I fucking envied you and your blacked out curtains and closed door and hidden life. But, look where it got you. And, look where I am now. I am friends with everyone - people just can't stop giving me promotions and bonuses. I am powerful. You are meek. You are the insect scuttling away from me and I am the fucking big bad bird of prey! Soaring the goddam skies taking what I want, when I want. You hide in your hole and I dominate the horizon. You had a couple of drinks and listened to some music and you thought you could have my life. You will never have my life. You will never enjoy because enjoyment is innate. You don't learn it and you don't search for it, it's inside you already.

But, watch me as I rule the world, as I suck it dry and scoop up all the rewards, while you scavenge the undergrowth in the darkness covered in shit looking for morsels; the crumbs of my excess. Don't you dare come back to the house. You are not welcome there anymore. I speak for all the housemates when I say this. We do not want you and you are not compatible with the way we want to live. You are on your own. I wanted to come here and tell you that nicely. I wanted it to be amicable. I wanted to apologise for throwing you out. But, look how you've made me act. Look at what you've made me say. This is not me. You turn me into something I am not. You make me act like you, all bitter and dried up inside. I wanted to be nice, I really did. Then, you blame us for putting you in hospital, you shit. Look how you've made me act. You had better savour your stay at the hospital, because when you get out, you'll have to find a hole to crawl into and live there instead. You fucking cockroach."

I didn't say a word back to him. I was shocked at his diatribe. I continued to stare at the ceiling, the bottomless infinity of white space sucking me in like a vortex. I was too ashamed to look him in the eyes. I heard him push his chair back and walk out of the ward. I heard him thank the nurses and say "goodnight" to them as he left.

I remained motionless. I hadn't realised that he despised me as much as I despised him. I began to think that maybe he was right about me. Maybe I was just an arrogant arsehole who thought I was something special because I looked down on the things that made others happy. The world was full of Guys and hardly any like me. So, by all accounts, that would make me the one who was in the wrong.

My mind went blank as I stared at the ceiling, allowing it to drag me into its emptiness. The whiteness surrounded me and completely enveloped my existence. I became one with the white darkness.

*

That night, my sleep was uneasy and restless. I woke in the middle of the night sweating and feverish. My mind was in a funk and I felt that something was wrong. I sat up. My head was spinning and I felt nauseous. I looked around the ward. The old woman next to me still had the curtain pulled around her bed. In fact, all the other patients had their curtains pulled too. So, why were mine still open? I looked for any nurses or doctors but I couldn't see any. The hospital had become a cavernous and desolate place. Had there been an evacuation and I left behind; forgotten or misplaced? Or, had I been left there on purpose, left to my own devices? Had the whole world been taken by Guy's words, believed his gospel, and left me in the hospital to rot away? Maybe Guy had organised this whole thing in order to deliver his final blow? One last act of punishment to show the world what would happen if they didn't follow his model of how life should be lived. He was making an example of me.

I couldn't bear the emptiness any longer. I shouted out to see if there was anyone around; I shouted out for a nurse, for the old woman, and for Jana, but no one heeded my calls. I began to sob. I felt completely alone. Abandoned in this place of recovery and death, knowing that even if I achieved the former, the latter would always be waiting. Why had the world forsaken me? Was I really so bad? Was I really that much of a threat to their way of life?

I screamed out again, but this time I screamed for the only thing that understood me, for the only thing that I understood: I screamed for the insects. I told them that I was sorry. I was sorry that I had abandoned them and sold them like cheap trinkets. I wanted them back; I wanted them to watch over me again. I was lost without them. I was alone without them. Come back to me.

An ant then appeared from nowhere and crawled up my bed sheet. I allowed it to scuttle up my finger and watched as it clung to my skin and explored the perimeter. Then, there were two ants on my finger. I didn't know where the second one had come from, but now it was there, jostling with the other ant. Soon, there were three ants, then four, then five, and soon there were too many to count. I was covered in a swarm. There were also beetles, cockroaches, flies, wasps, hornets, termites, crickets, and moths. All the insects that I could imagine were there. Thousands upon thousands of the things, all crawling over me, into my ears, into my mouth and even into my eye sockets. I could feel them all over my skin, inside my mouth, inside my mind. They were trying to devour me from within; to eat away at me from the inside out.

I tied to swat them away, but there were too many, and the more I swatted, the more they persisted. With a sudden surge of energy, I jumped out of bed, and in a frenzied state, I began scraping them off my body and spitting them out of my mouth. But they wouldn't stop. They continued their feast. I was their meal, and nothing was going to stop them from devouring me.

I rolled on the floor, screaming and desperately scratching every part of my body to free myself from their mandibles.

And that's how the nurses found me: rolling around deliriously on the hospital floor in a hallucinatory state. I swatted at the nurses as they tried to pick me up, thinking their fingers were the jaws of a million ravenous insects. I even drew blood from one of the nurse's arms. I had also succeeded in waking all the patients in the ward and probably some in the wards nearby too. My screams had echoed those of the old woman, a patient in the opposite bed delighted in telling me later.

I asked the nurse what could have sent me into such a state. She said that I had been through a traumatic experience and the memories of it could manifest themselves in a number of ways, but that was not for her to say, that was for the doctor to diagnose.

The doctor came by and checked me. He told me that it was just a bad dream and was nothing to worry about. He said to the nurse that I just needed some rest, and then he was gone. The nurse took my arm and injected a drug to help me "relax". It certainly helped me do that. I was out cold for the rest of the night. A dark sleep with no dreams or hallucinations. It was bliss.

*

The next morning, I awoke to find the old woman sitting up in her bed eating porridge. It was painful to watch. She would take the tiniest amount of porridge on her spoon and slowly move it towards her mouth, but her hands shook so much that the porridge would spill off the spoon and she would have to repeat the process. On the rare occasion that she did manage to get the porridge to her mouth, it would smear around her lips and get stuck to her toothless gums as she churned it around her mouth. She didn't seem to be swallowing any of it. Maybe some of it slid down her throat, but this was incidental and only a minimal amount was ingested. She noticed that I was watching her and turned her head to stare back at me with those huge, ghostly pale eyes. She didn't react to my disgusted countenance other than to return my gaze and continue to churn the porridge nonchalantly in her mouth as it dripped onto her chin and bed sheets.

I decided to try and talk to her, so I told her that last night I'd had a delirious dream in which I was being eaten alive by swarms of insects. I told her that it was the most vivid dream I had ever had, and I felt it as though it was actually happening to me; I could feel the insects eating my skin and flesh and crawling inside my ears. I could feel their antennae probing my body. I could taste them as they entered my mouth. I commented that it must have had something to do with all the drugs that they had injected into me, and then joked that in fact, it might have been due to the quality of the food that they served in the hospital. I said the mushy peas were bad enough to send anyone into a state of feverish delirium! The old woman remained unresponsive as she continued to swirl the porridge around her mouth. I then told her about Guy and how he had come to visit me to tell me that he was kicking me out of my house. I told her that I now had nowhere to live and no money, but I still had two weeks left until the next month's rent was due, so they couldn't evict me until then at least. She stared blankly and let the last bit of porridge in her mouth drip onto the bed. I told her that I didn't usually talk to anybody, but for some reason, I felt comfortable in her presence. I told her that her scream the previous day was like music and that it resounded in me. She made no reaction and turned her head away from me, beginning another attempt to eat the porridge. I said it was good talking to her and then I turned my head away to let her eat the rest of her breakfast in peace.

The hospital was chaotic. Nurses were rushing around, and the limited supply of doctors were struggling to perform the necessary checks on the patients. Finally, when a doctor came to check on me, I asked her how long she thought I would have to stay in the hospital. She told me it all depended on how well I recovered and that I had experienced a nasty head injury that needed monitoring. But, I could expect to be in there another few days at least. Then, she went away.

I didn't want to be in the hospital for any longer than necessary. I needed to be back at the house as quickly as I could to make sure I was inhabiting my room. I didn't want to give the others a chance to start showing it to any potential tenants. I needed to keep that room. I had no choice. It was that or be put out on the street.

I would get back to my room and go back to my old ways. I would just avoid everyone. Fuck them. I didn't care if they liked me or not, and I didn't want to give in to Guy so easily. I could not let him get away with this; he always got his way. I would stay in that room, find a shitty job and be a thorn in his side for the duration of my time in that house. If he wanted to be rid of me, then he would have to be the one to leave. Maybe I could get all those fuckers to move out.

I leant over to the old woman, who was staring off into the distance, and told her all about my plans and said that I was going to try and get out of this hospital as soon as I could find the opportunity. I had recovered sufficiently and didn't need to be there any longer. I told her that I was going to go back to my house and would do my best to ruin Guy's perfect little life. But, I didn't know where they had put my clothes. I asked her how I was going to get out of there without any clothes and no shoes. I asked her if she knew where they kept the clothes. She didn't respond and continued to stare blankly into the distance, her eyes fixed on nothing. I thought about it and then said to her that it didn't matter about the clothes and that I was just going to leave wearing whatever I could find.

I waited for the perfect moment when all the nurses and doctors were preoccupied, which did not take long, and climbed out of bed. Just as I was about to leave, I noticed that on the other side of the old woman's bed, a long coat was draped over the chair and a pair of her slippers were tucked under the bed. I took the slippers and tried them on for size. They were small for my feet, but at least they would be better than walking barefoot. I took her coat and put that on too. It was a slim fit, but again, it did its job and covered up my hospital gown.

I thanked the old lady for her kind gifts and she just chewed thin air while staring into space.

I made my way out of the hospital in the old woman's slippers, which were at least two sizes too small, and her long mac that was so tight it barely wrapped around me enough to zip up.

In the end, it wasn't hard to escape from the hospital anyway - no one cared if I was there or not. The nurses probably wouldn't even notice until lunchtime when they brought the meal.

As I walked through the hospital doors, I realised that I didn't have any money on me, my wallet being in my jeans pocket. I patted down the old woman's coat and turned out all the pockets; in the inside pocket, I found a crumpled five-pound note. I smirked and thanked the old woman again for her generous donations to my cause, and I swear I could hear her blistering scream emanating from the hospital as I walked to the street to find a bus. That deathly scream stayed with me forever.

*

I arrived back at the house after a long journey on the bus. My head was throbbing, and I wasn't really strong enough to be making a journey like that. Everyone on the bus stared at me; I must have been quite the sight in that old woman's attire and a ghastly suture across my head. But, I didn't care. Other people were of no consequence to me.

The only important thing was that I was back at the house. I stood outside the front door and wondered how I was going to get in. I didn't have my key, and I didn't want to ring the doorbell in case they wouldn't allow me to enter. Instead, I went to the alleyway that backed onto the house. I made my way through the alleyway and when I got to the back of the house, I peered over the fence to see if anyone was in the kitchen. It was empty. I climbed over the fence and every muscle and bone ached as I did so. I stopped in the garden for a second to allow the dizziness to subside and then continued to the back door. I was in luck - the door was unlocked. I slowly pushed it open and quietly went into the kitchen. I could hear the others. They were all in Loz's room whooping while playing a computer game. I didn't want to alert them to my presence yet; I firstly needed to get out of those clothes and make it look like I had been officially discharged from the hospital. I crept up the stairs while they played their game. I reached the door to my room and went inside. I stood there, first in confusion and then in shock - the whole room had been emptied. All my stuff was gone and all that remained was the bed and a bare wardrobe. What was going on? What had they done with my things? They must have already been showing it to potential tenants. I couldn't believe the audacity of it all. I knew that my things must be somewhere in the house, as they surely wouldn't have thrown it all away. I needed to find my stuff and put everything back in the room. I was not going to let them win that easily.

I came out of my room and saw that Guy's bedroom door was open. I went into his room, thinking that they might have stored my things in there. I rooted around in his cupboards and draws but there was no sign of my stuff, just all of Guy's boring shit. Then, I noticed that there was something stored under the bed: a big black bag. I pulled the bag out from under the bed and looked inside. The bag was full of the insects that I had sold to the online buyer. I stood there confusedly looking at the insects until it finally dawned on me that it was Guy who was the buyer all along. He had been playing me for a fool this entire time; getting me to give up all my things, and making me change who I was just so he could manipulate and then destroy me. Now, he was erasing my presence from the house completely. All my possessions gone. My room gone. The memory of me - gone.

I emptied out the bag and sorted through the insects - they were all there. I screamed out in anger. Then, shortly after, I heard the pounding of footsteps coming up the stairs - the housemates were on their way. Guy entered the room and saw me standing with the bag of insects.

"What are you doing?" he said calmly.

I was not as calm as Guy, though, and angrily demanded to know why he had told me to sell the insects and then proceeded to buy them for himself. Was he a fucking sociopath?

"I don't have to explain myself to you," he continued, just as calmly as before. "You need to vacate our house. Immediately."

Loz, Will, Oscar and Sean stood behind Guy and looked on with serious expressions. I guessed that they were trying to show that they were there to provide back-up for Guy if I were to attack him. I was heavily outnumbered.

I told Guy that I would not leave. I had two weeks left before the next rent was due and that I had up until then to find the next month's money.

"You don't live here," Guy said.

I told him that I was not going anywhere.

"You are a trespasser, and if you refuse to leave, I will call the police."

I questioned how I could be a trespasser when I had the legal right to be there. It was I who should call the police.

"Where's your contract then? Show me the contract or the proof that says that you should be here?" Guy said with a faint smirk.

I didn't have the contract. But, I told him that I could phone the landlord to confirm.

"The landlord won't do a thing," Guy said dismissively. "Do you know how I know that? Because I am going to be the new landlord of this house."

I stared at him blankly, unsure what he meant.

"I am negotiating to buy this place right now. I've been getting so much money at work that I thought I'd invest it, and what better way to do that than property? This house is the perfect investment."

I called him a cunt, to which he sniggered.

"And, do you know what landlords get to do? They get to choose who can live in their house."

In a sudden rush of rage, I lunged in to strike guy, but he easily deflected my attack. He simply dodged the punch and then pushed me to the floor. Guy laughed.

"So, I have a spare room," he said as I picked myself up off the floor. "It's quite nice. If you know of anyone that needs a room in a friendly houseshare, then do let me know. They would need to be outgoing, personable and like to have a good time. You wouldn't happen to know of anyone like that, would you?"

I lunged at him again and swung a wild punch at his jaw. He caught my fist and twisted my arm behind my back. I yelped in pain.

"But, we must let any potential tenant know," he said as he twisted my arm tighter, "that we did have one hell of an insect problem in that room. However, we did get the exterminator in and he's done a very good job of killing them." He gave my arm one final twist before throwing me back to the floor again. "Problem is, there does seem to be one insect left though. It's a real bugger to exterminate. A real, stubborn bit of vermin, this one. But, rest assured, we are doing everything in our power to exterminate that one, too."

I scuttled on all fours over to Guy and sunk my teeth into his leg. He screeched in pain. I made clicking sounds with my jaw and pressed the backs of my hands up against my brow and made twitching motions with my fingers as if they were antennae.

"This fucker is insane! Grab him!" Guy screamed and gestured to the others to incapacitate me.

I squirmed and shrieked as they pinned me to the floor. They took hold of my limbs and lifted me up. They carried me downstairs as I continued to writhe violently, trying to free myself from their grip. But, they were much stronger than me and easily fought against my feeble attempts. I was like a beetle trapped in a cup. They took me to the front door, opened it and dropped me onto the concrete path outside. I fell with an agonising impact. One of the stitches on my head opened up and the wound began to bleed. I looked back at the house through my now blurred vision. They were all stood there blockading the door. There was no way I was going to be able to make it back into the house. I crawled off into the street and disappeared into some undergrowth in a nearby park. I hid there in a damp thicket. I had nowhere else to go. My head was bleeding, so I picked up a handful of mud and caked it over my forehead to plug the wound. It was effective, and the blood soon stopped pouring. I was cold, so I proceeded to writhe around in the mud to cover my whole body. Soon, I was completely caked from head to toe. It began to rain, and I slithered deeper into the bushes to take shelter. The bristles of the bushes scraped and pricked my skin; I felt the pain, but it didn't bother me. The rain brought the molluscs to the surface and being hungry, I instinctively grabbed a snail and sucked it out of its shell. I didn't think of taste or texture as I swallowed it whole. My disgust reflexes were now non-existent, and a snail might as well have been a fine-dining meal at a Michelin star restaurant. To me, it was all the same. When I had eaten all the snails that I could find, I laid down in the saturated mud and looked up at the sky as the rain poured down on my body. I no longer questioned how my life had led me to this point. I didn't try to understand anything, and I didn't yearn for any form of materialism. Why should I judge myself by human standards and morality, when I did not identify with them anyway? To me, they were just as blank and as impenetrable as the dead insects that once sat on my shelves. Only, this time, I realised that they were not watching over me; not the insects, nor humanity nor anything else. No-one was watching me, no one was observing me, no one was judging me. I was, like every other creature, completely alone. And, it was at that point that I had never felt so free.

*

When I awoke, the rain had stopped, but the ground was still wet and slippery. My body was still covered in mud and the wound on my forehead was throbbing intensely. I was also starving. I needed food. I rooted around the undergrowth to see if I could find anything to eat, but all I found were leaves and dirt. I had no money, so I couldn't buy any food, but I did know of one place where I could get my hands on something to eat.

I picked myself up off the floor and stood up. My head was dizzy and I couldn't walk straight so I fell back down on my hands and knees. Fuck it, if I couldn't walk, then I would crawl. I crawled out of the park and back onto the street. I could sense that there were people around me on the street mocking me and staring at me in disgust as I crawled, half-naked, covered in mud and blood and mumbling incoherently. I took no notice of them, though. I was an insect now, and I didn't need their approval or revulsion. Nothing they did or thought was of any consequence to me.

I eventually made it to the alleyway that backed onto Guy's house, climbed over the fence and crawled to the back door. I tried to open the door, but this time it was locked and wouldn't budge. I rattled it back and forth to try and force it open, but it was locked tight. I searched the garden for a rock or a stone, but the garden was bare. I then noticed that the dividing wall to the garden next door had a few loose bricks. I jiggled one of them until it came free. I took the brick and threw it through the glass panel in the back door. The glass shattered and gave me an opening through which I put my arm and unlocked the door.

I was in the kitchen. I began to rummage through the fridge and all the cupboards, picking out bits of food which I took one bite of before discarding the remainder on the floor. I tore apart a whole box of cereal, ate one flake and then threw away the rest. I took a chunk out of an apple and dropped it straight after. I took a sip of juice and then poured the rest of the carton over the cooker. By the time I was finished, the place was a mess; every single item of food from the cupboards and fridge were now spread across the kitchen. I got back on my hands and knees and began to nibble the food off the floor.

"What the fuck are you doing?" I heard Guy scream.

I looked up and there he was with Loz and Will. I clicked my mouth at him.

"He's gone fucking insane!" Guy continued. "Let's grab him, Loz. Will, you call the police."

Loz dived in to grab me and I scurried out of the way. I clicked my mouth at him to ward him off. He started for me again, but he slipped on the food and fell on the floor. Guy poised his arms ready to grab me, but I watched him closely and backed out of the way.

"Don't worry, I'll get you," Guy said. "I'll get you. You dirty little fucker. You vile, feral piece of shit."

I picked up the cardboard cereal box off the floor and held it in my hand. Guy looked at me curiously.

"What do you think you are going to do with that? That's not going to protect you," he said.

I quickly lit the hob and put the cardboard over it, setting the box on fire. It blazed in my hand. I made more aggressive clicking noises with my mouth.

"Hey, man. Careful with that," Guy said, suddenly becoming concerned.

The cardboard box was now fully ablaze. I looked Guy deep into his hollow eyes and sneered at him. I then placed the fire on the floor, which in turn caused the detritus to light up. Soon, the floor was also ablaze.

"Get the fire extinguisher!" Guy screamed.

But, there was no extinguisher in the kitchen. It hadn't been replaced since the last time that I had used it. The housemates were now panicking and running around wildly, trying to find something to extinguish the fire.

I saw that the fire was expanding rapidly and getting out of control, so I scuttled out of the back door and jumped over the fence and into the alleyway. I peered back over the fence and watched as the fire consumed the whole kitchen. Guy, Loz, and Will escaped out of the front door. They were shouting hysterically and flailing their arms in disarray.

Smoke billowed from the windows and filled the air, creating a dense grey smog. Soon, I couldn't see anything except the smoke. I crawled out from the alleyway and back to the street. I hid behind a car and watched as people began to gather to watch the blazing house. They pointed and looked on, enjoying the spectacle. I heard the sound of sirens in the distance.

I saw Guy, Loz, and Will watching the house burn. Loz and Will watched in amazement at what they were seeing, while Guy paced up and down, punching the air angrily with tight fists, his empire in ruins before him. I stared at him and realised that I should have felt some enjoyment in my victory, but I didn't. Perhaps I should've felt guilt, but I didn't feel that either. I felt nothing. A fire was a fire, and Guy's house and possessions were part of that fire. That was all. It was all the same thing.

A fire engine arrived, closely followed by a police car and an ambulance. The firemen began to tackle the blaze while Guy hysterically explained to the policemen what had happened. I couldn't hear most of what he was saying, but at one point, he shouted so loud and clear that it resounded through the whole street. He said, "He thinks he's a fucking insect! He's out of his goddam mind!"

When I heard that, I knew it was time to get out of there. I turned and began to scuttle off down the street. An onlooker saw me and instantly recognised me from Guy's manic statement to the police. He shouted back to Guy and the police officers, alerting them all to my presence.

I heard Guy shout "Yes! That's him. The bastard!" Then, I heard the sound of heavy shoes clattering on the ground as the police began their pursuit. They soon caught up with me and wrestled me to the ground. I squirmed and shrieked with a high-pitched wail. I bit one of the policemen on the hand and he returned the favour by coshing me over the head.

I blacked out.

*

The next thing I knew, I was back at the hospital. But, this time, I was being guarded by a police officer who was sitting close to my bed. When he saw that I was awake, he called his colleague and they both questioned me about the events. My head was still dazed, and I answered their questions only with clicks, shrieks and wild limb spasms. I was an insect and did not conform to their laws or morals, so I would not answer to them.

The police officers looked at each other and they concluded that I was mentally unstable.

Soon after leaving the hospital, I underwent numerous mental health checks and was then tried in court for arson. Guy made an appearance to testify. When the barrister asked him to describe my personality, Guy said that he had prepared a statement and asked if he could read it. The judge agreed. Guy read out his statement: "When I first met Nilos, I knew something was not right about him. He was reclusive and unresponsive to positive advances. He never wanted to socialise or converse with the other housemates. He prided himself on being an outcast. He compulsively kept to his room and obsessed over insects. Insects were the only thing he could relate to, and he had no time for humans. As the time passed in the house, his behaviour became increasingly irrational and strange. He did not enjoy anything: food, films, books, sport, music, style, fashion, comedy, travel, art, clubs, pubs. Nothing. There has to be something suspicious about a man that cannot find enjoyment in anything. Doesn't there? Is he even a man? He lacks a simple human component. A man who cannot enjoy is no better than a base creature purely driven by instinct. He is no better than an insect that you would crush under your foot without even noticing or sparing a thought for. He is an insect wrapped in human skin. That is all he is. I now feel no ill feelings towards him, even though he burnt down our home, our sanctuary, my house. I wish him the best. But, he is unstable. He is not one of us. He has no dreams or desires. How can a man be born without such simple human qualities? Where is his spirituality? The yearning to be more than he is? To rise above the other creatures? To realise that he is part of a species that is the greatest to ever set foot on this earth? We transcend the other creatures and bear minimal similarity to their condition. Nil does not belong to our society. He caused significant damage by being part of a society to which he does not belong, that he is not a part of. If he does not understand the morals and boundaries of our society, then he should be taken from it until he learns. He has ruined my home. Our home. He needs to understand what he has taken from us. He needs to be taken away from us. I wish him all the best and I hope he recovers, but until then, he needs to be removed from society at all costs. He is a threat to our way of life. We cannot accept his way of life. We cannot accept him. I am not a vindictive man, so I will concede that Nilos is mentally ill. I will not say otherwise to try and punish him to the fullest. But, he must be rehabilitated at all costs. We cannot tolerate a person who cannot relate to our human condition. That is my statement. I thank you for listening."

What a load of bollocks, I thought. Anyway, I didn't care if I was imprisoned or not. I didn't even know why I had to go through the trial, as I had already pleaded guilty. The trial was more about my mental stability than anything else. My court-appointed lawyer told me that it was all about proving that I was mentally unwell so they could reduce the sentence. I didn't really care either way. I had no use for the outside world anymore. Nevertheless, the judge found me to be mentally unwell and determined that I should be kept in a high-security psychiatric hospital, and that was that. I never saw Guy or the other housemates again.

*

A high-security hospital is much the same as a houseshare. It has the same limitations and the same aggravations, except that you don't have to pay for rent and food. Also, you don't have to pretend to like the people that you are sharing with and you're not required to enjoy anything. I don't dream of anything. The nights are black, and so are the days. Most of the time, I just stare into the middle distance and think of nothing at all. But, sometimes, just sometimes, Guy's court statement replays itself in my head. I can hear it word for word in my mind. His voice clear and concise, like I was hearing it live. At the time, I thought nothing of the statement. But, now it aggravates me. His self-importance and smugness dripped from every word and now I want to have my chance to respond to him. This is my response:

"Guy, you said in your statement that enjoyment, desire, and dreams were an innate quality that was bestowed upon us humans; that without these simple things, a subject would fail to be a human at all. Do you really think that we are born with an appreciation of film or music or fancy foods? Can you honestly say that you came out of the womb with a desire to drink organic coffee while watching a French film? I say that we are born as nothing. We enter the world from a void and return to the void after our lives. We are, in essence, that very void from which we are conceived, and everything else is just a layer that sits over the top covering that void: a layer of bullshit to hide the truth that lies at the core.

I would love to know, Guy, why you think the ability to enjoy a craft beer puts the human condition above the creatures with whom we share this planet. You are a spiritualist who believes that the power of consumerism will elevate us above our station. That is your religion. You don't merely consume the material product, you consume the intangible notions that give meaning to that product. You consume enjoyment. You consume individualism. You consume desire itself. And, you are doomed to consume forever as these concepts are impossible to fulfil. The *idea* of enjoyment is what you experience, not enjoyment itself. Consumerism is intertwined with every facet of our lives and culture and has become the very framing of our reality. You do what the adverts say, you sing the lyrics that they tell you to sing, you dance the moves that they show you to dance, you watch TV and cry and laugh at the bits they prompt you to cry and laugh at. All the while, you pretend that you're an individual while you are doing it.

Before I met you, I was content with my lack of agency, my detachment from culture, and my indifference to society. I did not need the world that you inhabited, the world that you adored. But, you could not bear to see a person subvert your ideals, and you could not stand by while someone exposed the inconsistencies that existed at the core of what you inherently believed. I was a threat to you and your way of life. So, you sought to destroy me by giving me a taste of your world. You thought you could persuade me to see how sweet the lies could be. But, you failed. Your world is hollow. It is dull and insipid. And, you have known this all along. This is why you strain so hard to prop up the fiction that your world is great, because, without the alluring lies, the truth is exposed in all its naked horror.

You said that you despised my insects, but I know you were intrigued and even morbidly fascinated by them. The disgust and inconsistency you felt towards them was the most enjoyment you had ever experienced. That is why you ultimately had to own them all.

We are no better and no worse than those insects or tiny creatures that live in their millions beneath our feet. We are not the same, but neither are we different. Nothing matters, and nothing is nothing. Sentience, desires, dreams, a functioning society - they are all just fictions. You, Guy, are also a fiction, as am I, as are the insects that we categorise for our own sense of superiority. The difference is that your fictions are more persuasive, and that's why I am in here and you are out there.

Do you remember the time, Guy, when you first came to the house and you made that paella with the other housemates? Well, while you were making that meal, I was listening from upstairs. I pretended to myself that I wasn't curious about how that paella tasted. I remember how delicious you all said it was, and how you all revelled in the process of cooking it. I knew I had to try that paella, to see what you were all raving about. So, I crept downstairs that night, went to the fridge and tried some of the leftovers. I tasted it, full of anticipation. And, I'll tell you something, Guy, that paella tasted nothing like you all said it did. It tasted like the vacuous lies you all tell each other every day. After all the ways you tried to spruce it up with herbs and spices and fresh ingredients, it ultimately just tasted like a bland bowl of rice. And that's all your fucking life is.

Printed in Great Britain
by Amazon